EMMA'S BOOK

EMMA'S ISLAND

Honor Arundel wrote her first children's book to entertain her two youngest daughters who wanted to read about ordinary children in ordinary circumstances. The book was a great success and Miss Arundel went on to write a number of novels for children. She lived in Scotland until her death in 1973.

In *Emma's Island*, Aunt Patsy marries an artist friend and they move to a remote Scottish island. Having learnt to love living in Edinburgh, Emma is loathe to leave, but soon adapts to island life and even has her first taste of romance.

The first book in the 'Emma' series, *The High House*, and the third, *Emma in Love*, have also been published in Piccolo.

D0566669

Also by Honor Arundel in Piccolo

THE HIGH HOUSE
EMMA IN LOVE

HONOR ARUNDEL

EMMA'S ISLAND

Cover illustration by Mary Dinsdale

A Piccolo Book

PAN BOOKS
LONDON AND SYDNEY

First published 1968 by Hamish Hamilton Ltd
This edition published 1972 by Pan Books Ltd,
Cavaye Place, London SW10 9PG
2nd printing 1976
© Honor Arundel 1968
ISBN 0 330 23218 5

Made and printed in Great Britain by
Cox & Wyman Ltd, London, Reading and Fakenham

This book is sold subject to the condition that it
shall not, by way of trade or otherwise, be lent, re-sold,
hired out or otherwise circulated without the publisher's prior
consent in any form of binding or cover other than that in which
it is published and without a similar condition including this
condition being imposed on the subsequent purchaser

For Claude, Jill and Ruth

Chapter One

'EMMA!' Aunt Patsy called plaintively. 'Oh, Emma! We've run out of bread.'

'Oh no.'

'I thought today was the day the van called. Isn't it Wednesday?'

'No,' I said fiercely, 'it's Tuesday. You're a day out. I knew what would happen if you came to live on an island.'

We stared at each other and began to laugh.

'Please, Emma, dear Emma,' coaxed Aunt Patsy.

'But it's raining.'

'Not much,' Aunt Patsy said, looking at the streaming windows.

'Can't Stephen go?'

'You know he's busy transforming the barn.'

I knew I should have to go, so sighing and grumbling I put on my oilskins while Aunt Patsy hovered apologetically.

'Buy yourself some chocolate,' she said, giving me money from her purse.

'And a Coke?'

'Oh, all right. You drive a hard bargain.'

I wheeled my bike out of the shed and set off for the shop at Ardloch two miles away.

People who think life on a small island is simple are quite wrong. It is extremely complicated. In a town the milk arrives on your doorstep in a bottle; on an island you have to find a neighbour who keeps cows and collect it yourself in a milk can. In a town if you need an electrician or a plumber you ring one up; on an island you have to find a man who knows a man who may have time next Thursday week if the weather is fine. In a town you nip out to the shops and buy whatever you want and have the money for; on an island you have to order things in advance, so on Thursday you have to make up your mind what sort of meat you will want to eat on Sunday. Aunt Patsy, of course, found this almost impossible to do and we got very sick of tinned luncheon meat and beans. If you want fish you do not go to the fishmonger because there isn't one, you find out when Hamish or Dougal or Ian is going out in his boat and lie in wait for him on his return.

And all these arrangements have to be made over a great deal of conversation, cups of tea or drams of whisky.

But we were new to the island and it took us some time to discover all these niceties. In fact we had only been there for two weeks.

It had been quite a wrench to leave the High House in Edinburgh. I had come, like Aunt Patsy, to feel it was special and exciting to live on a flight of steps instead of in a proper street and to be able to see out of our windows the Castle, the hills, the Firth of Forth and all the black chimneys smoking busily in the city below. Aunt Patsy and I used to jeer at those of our friends who arrived panting at our front door, exhausted from climbing the sixty-eight dusty stone stairs – we never panted even when we had to carry heavy loads of shopping – and say airily: 'The stairs? Oh, we never notice them.'

But the place had become more than a little cramped since Aunt Patsy had married Stephen, because he was an artist, too, and needed room for all his painting gear, not to speak of his books. It was lucky he did not have many clothes as where he would have kept them I don't know. The result was that poor Stephen's belongings were scattered round the house in the most unlikely places so that we were always tripping over piles of books or shoes and Stephen was always cursing because he could not find his portfolio or his umbrella or his pyjamas. Aunt Patsy's untidiness did not help and I was often thankful that I had my own room, spick and span and properly organized, where I could read and do my homework in peace.

Obviously we had to move. But a bigger house in Edinburgh would have cost too much and if we moved to the country, although Aunt Patsy, being a free-lance artist, could work more or less anywhere where there was a Post Office handy, Stephen would have had to give up his job as Art Editor of a magazine called *Scottish Homes*.

'I suppose there's no real objection to a man living off his wife's earnings,' said Stephen, 'but I'm an old-fashioned Scot and I don't fancy the idea. And I'm a little old to begin learning a new job like forestry or plumbing.'

'Anyhow,' said Aunt Patsy practically, 'I don't earn enough.'

'If only I had some rich relative who would die and leave me enough money to live in luxury and idleness,' complained Stephen.

Of course he did not really want to live in luxury and idleness, he wanted to paint, and after having a fairly successful exhibition during the winter he began to consider giving up his editing job and painting full-time.

If only we could find somewhere cheap to live.

This state of indecision lasted until one day in May, when I got back from school to find the two of them drinking coffee in the kitchen in a mood of wild excitement.

'Emma, we've found a cottage,' shouted Aunt Patsy almost before I had opened the door.

'On an island,' added Stephen.

'It's called Stranday and it's about two hours from Oban,' said Aunt Patsy.

'We're going to run a gallery,' said Stephen.

'Pots and gew gaws for tourist bait,' said Aunt Patsy.

'And pictures,' added Stephen.

'What?' I squeaked, falling into a chair.

'Cottage,' said Aunt Patsy.

'Island,' said Stephen.

They beamed at me happily.

'Tell me properly,' I begged, 'from the beginning.'

Stephen had just received a letter from a friend of his who had landed a good job in America. He owned a cottage on Stranday which he was willing to rent to us very cheaply for at least five years.

9

'We'll let this flat,' said Aunt Patsy. 'Oh, won't it be splendid? Living in a cottage by the sea.'

'Idyllic,' sighed Stephen.

'Idyllic, hmmmm,' I thought as I pedalled up the hill with the rain cascading down my face and finding its way into all the nooks and crannies that were theoretically guarded by swathes of oilskin.

Although a year and a half of living with Aunt Patsy had made me far less a creature of habit than I had been originally, I had known immediately that island life was not going to be idyllic. She and Stephen were wildly impractical about ordinary details of living. So when they started chattering about sunsets over the Atlantic, peat fires and long cosy evenings, I had immediately asked business-like questions.

'How big is the cottage?' I wanted to know. 'Has it got electricity and running water? Where's the nearest shop? What about my school? Is there a bus service?'

'You have no soul, Emma,' Aunt Patsy said sadly, 'no soul at all.'

'However, I shall indulge your appetite for practical details,' Stephen said. He took the letter from his pocket and began to read aloud:

'The cottage is about two miles from the jetty at Ardloch along the shore road to the west. It has two biggish rooms and a bathroom—'

'Good,' I interrupted.

'—on the ground floor,' continued Stephen, 'three bedrooms upstairs and a large floored barn that could be used as a studio. There's a solid fuel stove and electric light.'

'Hooray!'

'There's about half an acre of ground which I have never succeeded in cultivating, but perhaps your muscles are stronger than mine. Ardloch has a small hotel and a general purpose shop with a van that calls from time to time. There's no proper bus service but one of the islanders has a minibus that meets boats at the jetty and takes children to school. There are three boats a week but more during the tourist season. Don't forget waterproof clothing and bicycles.'

At that moment I had had a clear vision of myself in my wellingtons and oilskins cycling in the pouring rain because Aunt Patsy had forgotten to buy butter or bread or potatoes – and how right I had been.

'I wonder what the school's like,' I ruminated, 'and if it copes with O-levels.'

'Don't fuss, Emma. All schools are much the same. Anyhow,' added Aunt Patsy, who took a low view of education in general, 'you're almost fifteen – you could leave at any time.'

'I've no intention of leaving school,' I snapped, beginning a familiar argument, but Stephen quickly intervened.

'Now, now, girls. Of course Emma must go to school. Let's look at the atlas.'

I left them drooling over the map and went into my room to write to my brother Richard and tell him the news.

Richard is two years older than I am and intends to be a musician, either a composer or a conductor, he's not sure which. Although he is theoretically living with Aunt Laura in Exeter, he spends term-time in a rather enlightened boarding-school where they take music seriously. In the holidays he usually goes abroad to pick grapes or play the piano in cafés in any country where there is a music festival. In between he comes to Edinburgh and this was another reason why the High House got so cramped, because he had to sleep on the sofa in Aunt Patsy's studio.

Richard was not a creature of habit at all and I had no doubt that he would consider the island idea a splendid one, so after I had given him the news straight I went on:

'It is difficult enough to keep Aunt Patsy in order here but I'm sure on an island she will be even worse. Instead of being merely hours out, we shall probably be days and weeks out and end up celebrating Christmas at Easter. And I'll have to go to the village school and be taught by some ancient crone who has never heard of O-levels.

'I'm sure all this uprooting will be very bad for me psychologically. I'll probably become maladjusted and start biting my nails and screaming in the night. I foresee a grim summer.'

However I had gradually become used to the idea during the next few weeks when we had talked about nothing but the island. We studied it on the detailed map and looked at photographs, planned who would have which room, made and re-made our removal plans. We advertised the flat and a man from the Linguistics Department of the University, whom Aunt Patsy insisted upon referring to as Professor Pettifog, agreed to rent it for quite a generous monthly sum. Then Aunt Patsy and I went shopping to buy wellingtons, oilskins, huge jerseys and jeans. Stephen ordered bicycles to be sent direct from Oban.

I had learned that Stranday was a triangular-shaped island in a group with Coll and Tyree. Ardloch was in a bay just round the southern tip, our cottage was two miles to the west and the northern tip was a sort of nature reserve where there was a model farm and a deer forest. There were two quite high hills, 960 and 1,200 feet respectively, a small loch and a river. The population was 742.

I copied the map very carefully on to graph paper and stuck it on the wall in my room and studied it till I knew every detail, even with my eyes shut.

Of course Aunt Patsy had wanted to leave Edinburgh immediately but I insisted on waiting until term finished at the end of June.

'Who knows if I'll ever get any more proper education,' I grumbled, 'so I'm going to make the most of this last month. Besides, I don't want to miss Prize Giving.'

'You're not going to get a prize, are you?' asked Aunt Patsy with astonishment.

'Of course I am,' I replied smugly. 'Two actually, a class prize and a special history prize.'

'Good heavens. Do I have to come to this function?'

'You have to clap until your hands are sore,' I said, 'and be suitably dressed.'

'I'm not wearing gloves and a hat even to impress your friends,' Aunt Patsy snorted.

So the final arrangement was that Stephen would go ahead with most of the gear and the furniture that Professor Pettifog said he did not need, and that Aunt Patsy and I would follow with the rest the day after Prize Giving.

Packing was absolute murder. Special removal men had to lower the piano out of the window on a cable and arguments developed about what ought to be thrown away, what must be left for the Professor and what things we absolutely *must* have with us on the island. But somehow or other it got finished and Aunt Patsy and I were left alone in a strangely empty house. We received an ecstatic phone call from Stephen who reported that the cottage was fabulous, the island was fabulous, the people were fabulous. He'd been out fishing; he was painting the cottage; he was living on fish and whisky; there were one or two little problems but he'd have solved them before we arrived.

'What little problems?' I asked suspiciously – Aunt Patsy was kindly letting me share the telephone.

'Oh, you know, supplies mostly. The island's run out of potatoes. The old ones are finished and the new ones aren't ready yet and the boat didn't arrive yesterday because there was a storm.'

'Well, I hope it arrives on Thursday because we'll be on it,' said Aunt Patsy.

'I'll meet you at the jetty,' Stephen said, 'goodbye, my darlings. And bring a few spuds with you just in case.'

That last night we had hardly slept because we had been too excited and our train was due to leave at five o'clock in the morning. We had two suitcases each, a big naval duffel bag, left over from when Stephen was in the navy, full of coats and oilskins, a shopping-bag containing odds and ends with our favourite frying-pan sticking out at the top, a carrier bag full of potatoes and a rucksack stuffed with food for the journey.

We staggered down the stairs with this load, making two journeys each, and then we stood together at the top of the steps waiting for the taxi.

Just for a second I had felt a twinge of regret and I think Aunt Patsy did, too, because she squeezed my hand.

'Oh Emma,' she said, 'I hope Professor Pettifog of the Linguistics Department will appreciate living in the High House.'

Then the taxi arrived; we piled ourselves and our luggage into it and drove down the hill to Waverley Station.

How long ago it all seemed! For a year and a half the High House had been home and now suddenly home was a grey-stone cottage facing the Atlantic. The Emma who had trudged up and down the steps, who had lain awake at night listening to the wind, who had won the history prize at Park-hill school, seemed to be a quite different person from the one who now free-wheeled down the hill into Ardloch and anchored her bike outside the general purposes shop.

'Have you any bread left?' I asked Mr McDougall who was weighing sugar into pound packets while his two little boys were playing tennis (or houses) with the cardboard cartons. 'And I'll have a bar of Dairy Milk and a tin of Coke, please.'

Chapter Two

HALFWAY home the rain suddenly lifted; the clouds spun away leaving a great well of deep blue sky and the sea, which had been a sullen grey, turned into a sheet of smooth blue silk. The hedges, full of fuchsia, wild roses and foxgloves, sparkled with raindrops. The sun was hot so I got off my bike, removed my oilskins and stacked them on my carrier. I decided to have a breather and to eat my chocolate.

Two weeks ago Aunt Patsy and I had paused at this same spot, looking down into the green valley and guessing which one of the grey-stone cottages was ours. And I'd known im-mediately which one it was, a couple of hundred yards down a rough track, facing a sandy beach.

In spite of the fact that our journey had been full of mis-adventures and that we were both exhausted, we had spurted down the hill and positively galloped the last part of the track, yoo-hoo-ing for Stephen.

I still giggled at the memory of that journey.

This is what had happened:

We had arrived at Oban Station looking like emigrants –
'Or immigrants,' said Aunt Patsy. 'At this stage I suppose
we're both.'

A little grey rain was falling, making the platform grey
and slimy. Leaving Aunt Patsy with our suitcases, duffel bag
and various other articles of luggage strewn round her, I
went to look for a porter. At last I saw one, stout in his blue
overalls and with a bright pink face, so I dashed after him,
calling:

'Please could you help us with our luggage, we have to
catch the boat for Stranday.'

'Stranday? There's no boat for Stranday today.'

'What?' I yelped.

'There was one indeed, but it leaves at six o'clock on a
Thursday.'

'Six o'clock morning or six o'clock evening?'

'In the morning to be sure.'

'Oh no!' I bleated.

He waddled up the platform in a leisurely way and sur-
veyed our luggage.

'Aunt Patsy, he says there's no boat.'

'No boat? But there's supposed to be one at twelve. I
checked most particularly.'

'You have made a mistake,' said the porter cheerfully. 'Six
o'clock on a Thursday. You had better be inquiring at the
steamship office.'

He showed us the way to a small room, thick with ciga-
rette smoke, where a man was speaking on the telephone and
a girl was tapping a typewriter in a desultory way. Both of
them were drinking coffee.

Aunt Patsy explained our predicament as soon as the man
had finished with the telephone. He was extremely
interested and polite and took real pleasure in showing us the
schedules and pointing out triumphantly the boat we had
missed.

'Six o'clock Tuesdays, Thursdays and Saturdays,' he said
smiling.

'But they told me in Edinburgh—' began Aunt Patsy
feebly.

'Ah Edinburgh ... They'll have been thinking of the summer schedules.'

'But isn't it summer?'

'Summer schedules start next week.'

'Then when is the next boat?' I asked.

'Saturday.'

'Saturday?' Aunt Patsy and I gasped together shrilly.

'Aye, Saturday.' He put the schedules away and reached for his coffee cup.

For a moment I thought Aunt Patsy would explode with rage and tell him what she thought of him and the steamship company and British Railways and all officials everywhere. But she didn't. Her face drooped. Her beautiful grey eyes filled with tears. Her voice trembled.

'Please, please help us,' she pleaded. 'My niece and I must get to Stranday today – my husband's expecting us – he'll be terribly worried – we're going to live there, you see – oh dear, I don't know what to do.'

'Well now,' said the man thoughtfully.

'There's Hamish,' said the girl, suddenly becoming interested too.

'Is today not his trip to Jura?'

'It might be,' said the girl.

'I'll just see if he's left,' said the man and disappeared.

Aunt Patsy and I looked at each other despairingly. We were beyond speech.

In about ten minutes the man came back, beaming, accompanied by two enormous characters in jerseys, oilskins and sea boots.

'Where's the luggage?' asked one.

'Do you mean—' Aunt Patsy began.

'Aye, we'll take you to Stranday. The party says they don't mind. It'll make a nice round trip and in this weather it doesn't matter where they go.'

The steamship man explained that it would cost us five pounds because Hamish would have to go out of his way and we would need help to land the luggage at Stranday.

Quite dazed, Aunt Patsy and I shook hands with him, thanked him for his help and then followed the others to the quay where a small grubby boat was rocking uneasily at the bottom of an iron ladder.

'Oh Lord, have we got to climb that?' exclaimed Aunt Patsy. 'I hope you can swim, Emma.'

The two men threw our luggage down to the boat where it was expertly caught and stowed away. Then they helped us down the little ladder and swung us into the boat.

It was raining hard. There was a thick mist. The sea looked grey and wicked. I had a definite foreboding that I was going to be sea-sick.

Below deck was a sort of room where a dozen or so people were sitting, cheerful fat ladies in plastic macks, tough young camping types with bulging rucksacks, and the usual Americans with rimless glasses and huge cameras. They all smiled at us and assured us that they did not in the least mind going to Stranday to drop us off. The engine began to chug into violent life; the boat moved off; a girl produced mugs of tea out of a cubby-hole. Aunt Patsy and I relaxed and grinned at each other.

'What did you think of my little woman act in the steamship office?' she asked slyly.

'It took me in completely,' I admitted.

'Well, I decided to test this highland chivalry we're always hearing about. Do you want to go on deck?'

I poked my nose out and a gust of wind nearly sliced it off. The rain and the mist were so thick I could see nothing except the nasty slapping waves so I decided it would be better to stay below. I did feel a little queasy but as I was also extremely tired, I luckily fell asleep before I had time to be sick.

The next thing I knew was Aunt Patsy saying excitedly: 'Emma, it's stopped raining. Come and look at our island.'

I scrambled on deck after her and we gazed and gazed across the greeny-grey sea at a greeny-grey island, our island: high cliffs, rocks, grey and white houses; a mountain in the distance scarfed with mist; sheep like mushrooms in the grass; flocks of gulls miaowing like cats.

I would never forget that moment. The first time I had

seen Edinburgh I had hated it bitterly, it was so cold and grey and unfriendly, but Stranday was somehow my island right from the start.

Hamish at the tiller beckoned us over.

'It's low tide so I'll not be able to anchor at the jetty,' he said. 'I will put you ashore in the dinghy.'

Now we could see the jetty quite clearly and the houses in the distance that must be Ardloch. Our boat, *The Island Queen*, slowed down and stopped. The girl who had made the tea jumped recklessly into the dinghy while Hamish and the other man dropped our luggage into it. The little boat sank lower and lower. Then it was my turn and I did not fancy it at all. I hate steep slippery ladders, especially when they do not even keep still. The dinghy, too, was bobbing about in the most alarming way. I gulped and looked appealingly at Aunt Patsy but there was nothing that either of us could do about it. So I gritted my teeth, wished I was as good at rock climbing as my brother Richard, and began to lower myself nervously from rung to rung. Then miraculously I was in the boat; Aunt Patsy followed and all the passengers in *The Island Queen* leaned over the side to wave and cheer and wish us a happy landing.

The girl rowed us expertly towards the jetty and there was yet another steep seaweedy ladder to climb – only this one, thank goodness, was stationary. I got out first for Aunt Patsy and the girl to pass up the luggage to me. Then I gave my hand to Aunt Patsy who seemed to dislike this ladder even more than the last one. At last we stood together, among our luggage, exhausted but triumphant.

'We've arrived,' said Aunt Patsy.

The girl pushed off, saying, 'You'd better ring Donald about the luggage,' and rowed briskly away.

We realized then that although we *had* more or less arrived there were still what Stephen would have called one or two little problems to solve.

Because of our unscheduled arrival there was no one to meet us, no Stephen, no minibus for the luggage, and there was no way of getting to our cottage except on foot.

The jetty was bare except for a freight shed so, as a start, we dragged our gear there. Inside was a telephone and we both eyed it thoughtfully till I said jokingly:

'You'd better ring Donald.'

'All right, I will.'

'But you don't even know his name.'

'I know he drives the minibus. Anyhow, what can I lose except sixpence?'

So Aunt Patsy dialled the operator and said:

'I'm ringing from the jetty at Stranday and I want to speak to the Donald who drives the minibus.'

She reported back to me triumphantly. 'She says Donald is at the north of the island delivering stores but she'll give him a message when he gets back. We can leave our stuff here.'

'I shall take the potatoes with me,' I said firmly.

'The thing is, Emma, shall we go to the hotel at Ardloch to get something to eat or go direct to the cottage?'

'The cottage – if we can find it,' I said. I couldn't wait.

So we had set off up the path from the jetty and when it joined the main – and only – road we turned left along the shore where I was bicycling today. Presently the road rose steeply through rough moorland and the sea disappeared. There was not a cottage in sight.

'I suppose we are going in the right direction,' said Aunt Patsy uneasily.

'Of course.'

Just then a man in working overalls overtook us on a bicycle and Aunt Patsy flagged him down.

'I wonder if you could tell us—' she began.

'You'll be Mrs McTaggart,' he interrupted smiling, 'you'll see your cottage when you get to the top of the brae – it's the first one on the left, facing the sea. The man was expecting you on the morning boat.'

'Well, you see—' Aunt Patsy started feebly to explain, but he just smiled as he swung his leg over the bicycle and called back over his shoulder:

'About a mile, you cannot miss it. Good day to you.'

So we trudged up the hill and down the other side and over a little grey-stone bridge spanning a peat-brown burn and then the sea reappeared and there was a wide green glen scattered with crofts.

How marvellous it had been when Stephen came rushing out to meet us, saying: 'You missed the boat, you silly clots. I've been worried stiff,' and hugged us both.

And Aunt Patsy and I had both started explaining at the same time and suddenly it had all appeared terribly funny. We spluttered with laughter; we choked and giggled; we rocked to and fro until Stephen began to laugh too and said: 'What? He didn't! Good Lord! You don't mean it,' at intervals.

He had led us into the kitchen where a good fire was burning and Aunt Patsy sank into a ramshackle armchair, wiping her eyes. 'Pour me immediately a large glass of whisky,' she gasped, 'put the kettle on and prepare your finest viands. We're starving and exhausted as well as being nervous wrecks.'

'There's a little problem here,' Stephen hinted, 'still no potatoes.'

This had been my opportunity.

'Problem solved,' I said grandly, 'I have brought the potatoes.'

'Wonderful Emma.'

Yes, I had been a great help to them, I thought smugly, as I climbed back on to my bicycle and cruised gently down the road to the cottage. In fact they could hardly have managed without me.

Chapter Three

It surprised me to find that I enjoyed life on the island more than in Edinburgh. The High House had always been Aunt Patsy's but the cottage was somehow mine, too. I did not have to fit into someone else's way of life since we were all evolving a new one together.

The cottage was just the right size for us. We had one all-purpose room for cooking, eating and sitting in and one civilized room for playing records and having intelligent conversation in. But naturally during those first weeks we had no time for playing records or having intelligent conversation so the civilized room was just used to store all the things that later would go into the gallery. Upstairs were two medium-sized bedrooms and one small one – 'For Richard when he comes to stay,' I thought with satisfaction.

We all worked like – I was going to say slaves but slaves did not enjoy their work and we did. I made curtains, painted the bathroom and my own room, arranged the kitchen gear, cooked, washed up and biked endlessly into Ardloch for stores. Stephen put windows in the barn, dug the garden and went fishing. Aunt Patsy helped with the barn, painted the front door a beautiful dark blue, cooked and even managed to do a little of her own work.

Every now and again she would say:

'I feel like bright lights and sweet music,' and we would bike down to the Ardloch Hotel for lunch or supper. (There were no bright lights or sweet music but at any rate we did not have to cook or wash up.) Or she would say:

'I'm going mad. What is this life if full of care?' and go off by herself for long walks along the shore where she could stare as far as she liked without seeing anything except sea.

Sometimes Stephen and I went with her. We were lucky to have our sandy beach only fifty yards from the cottage and I loved walking along barefoot through the small crinkly waves, looking for driftwood. Occasionally Stephen and I swam but Aunt Patsy said she did not believe this nonsense about the Gulf Stream – she was convinced the water flowed straight from the Arctic Circle.

Of course little problems continued to arise and then we would have a family council and I enjoyed finding ingenious ways out of our difficulties.

One little problem was that of not having fresh vegetables. The shop hardly bothered to stock them, partly because most islanders grew enough for their own needs, and partly because freight charges made them so expensive.

But since our garden was still a wilderness, all we had were expensive tomatoes from the shop, the odd cauliflower or lettuce that someone had grown too many of, and endless carrots. Otherwise we had to stick to tinned peas, and beans.

This was when I discovered nettles.

'The book says they taste like spinach,' I said happily.

'Nettles?' exclaimed Aunt Patsy.

'I don't care what they taste like. I'd rather get scurvy than eat nettles,' said Stephen.

'Don't be so reactionary,' snapped Aunt Patsy.

'The books says you can eat seaweed too,' I added.

'I'm not going to eat seaweed,' shouted Stephen, stamping out of the house to go and dig the garden.

Aunt Patsy looked at me and sighed. 'Honestly, Emma, if I have to eat another tinned pea I shall turn into one myself. What do you say we experiment? We won't tell Stephen. Show me what the book says.'

So when Stephen had gone off on his bike to Ardloch to see a man about glazing the windows in the barn – which we now called the gallery – Aunt Patsy and I put on our woollen gloves and set out for a field behind the house where nettles grew.

'Ugh, they do look rather nasty,' she said, 'just pick the green young ones, Emma.'

So we filled a basket with nettles and then Aunt Patsy washed them thoroughly, put them in a saucepan with a little butter and hoped for the best. Like spinach, they disintegrated rather quickly so that our huge panful turned into barely enough for three.

She served it with corned beef and – at last – new potatoes for supper.

'What's this?' asked Stephen suspiciously.

'Spinach,' said Aunt Patsy, taking a big forkful and munching happily.

'Is it, Emma?' asked Stephen.

'Why ask me?' I prevaricated. I was not very keen on trying it either but I took a small mouthful and tried to look ecstatic. 'Delicious,' I mumbled.

Stephen took the minutest bit and tasted it with the tip of his tongue.

'Nettles,' he accused us. 'I know it's nettles. Ugh!'

'What nonsense, darling,' said Aunt Patsy smoothly.

But it was no good. He would not touch them.

'You'll get scurvy and your teeth will drop out,' she pointed out.

Another little problem was the piano. It had simply not arrived. Aunt Patsy and Stephen went into Ardloch where the nearest telephone was, armed with pocketfuls of shillings and sixpences, to ring up the steamship company, British Railways, British Road Services, the removal company and anyone else they could think of, but nobody knew what had happened to it.

'It's probably sitting in some freight yard getting water-logged or eaten by rats,' said Aunt Patsy gloomily.

'Or perhaps there's some musical porter who gives nightly recitals of Beethoven?' said Stephen.

'I think we should ask Donald,' I suggested. 'He's bound to know a man who knows a man who knows a musical porter.'

So we asked Donald and the next time he went to Oban he poked around the sheds and funnily enough there *had* been a musical porter who, worried about the piano getting wet, had had it moved to an inner shed and then forgotten about it.

By the time it really did arrive everyone on the island knew about it and there was a great cheer when it was hoisted on to the jetty. And there were dozens of volunteers to lift it on to the trailer which a tractor man used for de-livering coal and farming equipment.

It would not go into the cottage – that was a foregone conclusion, the porch being too narrow and the windows too small – so we had it placed in the gallery.

'Richard can give recitals here,' said Aunt Patsy.

Stephen hoped to open the gallery in August before all the tourists went away. He had pictures of his own and by young artist friends of his; then there were Aunt Patsy's tiles and some nice pottery pendants hung on leather thongs. She had also dashed off some pen-and-wash drawings of the island at a guinea each for what she called contemptuously 'tourist bait'. Frankly I liked them much better than Stephen's peculiar pictures. A consignment of pottery made by one of Stephen's students at the Edinburgh Art College (he used to teach there part-time) was expected any day. I wished I had been artistic, too, but all I could do was to help arrange things and laboriously type out copies of the catalogue.

The last week was one mad rush. We managed to borrow some trestle tables from the church hall to display the pottery and we hung the pictures on the roughly white-washed walls. The cement floor we had to leave in its original state but at least it was clean. It had needed seven maids with seven mops, as Aunt Patsy said, but the three of us had had to do the work of seven, wearing out several scrubbing-brushes in the process.

'Neat but not gaudy,' said Stephen, 'next year we'll get some sisal matting.'

On the Friday evening there was going to be a private view for critics and friends; then on the Saturday the gallery would be open for the general public. So we booked rooms at the hotel for the critics and looked out lilos and blankets for the friends who might be staying overnight.

Two of Stephen's ex-students arrived, Jim and Dave, and though they were a great help they ate an enormous amount and this made things difficult for Aunt Patsy and me. We used to make great panfuls of soup into which we surreptitiously put chopped nettles.

'What the eye doesn't see,' said Aunt Patsy.

In the middle of all this we had a message via the Ardloch Hotel and the postman that Richard was coming.

'Yes, go and meet the boat,' Aunt Patsy said when she saw my reaction to the news – I had nearly embraced the postman.

'Are you sure you can manage?'

'Indubitably.'

So I biked down to the jetty and waited with all the other people for the steamer. Anyone who had nothing more important to do always met the steamer. It was the big event of the day. Already we seemed to know a lot of people who had all heard that my brother was arriving and made friendly remarks to me.

When the steamer stopped and was met by the small island boat, I could see Richard's copper nob quite clearly and he managed to be one of the first people to land.

'Richard!' I yelped in my most undignified manner, flinging my arms round him, but luckily he did not mind.

'I thought I'd better investigate this island retreat of yours.'

'Oh, I'm so glad you've come.'

We walked away from the jetty, me wheeling my bike and Richard humping his rucksack.

'I say, you *have* turned into an outdoor girl,' he said, looking me up and down. 'I can hardly recognize you.'

It was true, though I had not noticed it myself before. I always used to be short-haired and neat and tidy. Now my hair had grown because Aunt Patsy and I had not yet discovered anyone who knew anyone who cut hair and the salty air and the wind made tidiness totally impossible. My jeans had streaks of paint on them, my big toe had made its way through one of my sneakers, my jersey was far from spotless.

'Is a highland cattle hair-cut the new fashion?' inquired Richard.

'Well,' I said.

Naturally we had a lot of news to exchange and we were still talking like maniacs after supper round the fire.

So we did not notice the storm until it broke. Certainly the wind had been rising all day and the waves had been rolling up the beach like great silvery monsters as the tide came in. But now the rain started rattling on the windows like marbles and there were great rumbles of thunder.

During a break in the conversation we listened to the noise of the storm and congratulated ourselves on being snugly indoors.

'Nothing like two feet of stone between us and the elements,' said Stephen. 'All the same, I think I'd better check that the gallery is all right.'

He put on his oilskins and gum-boots and disappeared as if he were being sucked into a whirlpool. He was back in a couple of minutes.

'All hands wanted,' he shouted, 'the roof's leaking. Bring pots and basins.'

We dashed for our rainwear and stumbled, fighting our way through wind and rain, to the gallery. There were sinister puddles on the floor into which the rain steadily plopped. Jim and Dave moved their lilos and sleeping-bags; Aunt Patsy and I moved the trestle tables on which the pottery was displayed; Stephen took down some of the pictures; Richard began to shove the piano but it was too big not to catch some of the drips, so he dried it lovingly and covered it with his mack.

We put bowls and pots and saucepans under the worst drips and mopped up the floor.

'Oh Lord, where are you going to sleep?' moaned Aunt Patsy to Jim and Dave, because there did not seem enough dry floor anywhere. 'You'll have to come back and camp out in the cottage.'

'I know,' said Richard, 'put them under the piano and we'll arrange the macks on top.'

'Brilliant,' said Stephen.

So that was what we did and then we bolted back into the kitchen, a little giggly because Jim and Dave looked so funny under the piano.

'Is life on the island always like this?' inquired Richard, on our way to bed after our usual late-night gossip.

'Always,' I said.

Chapter Four

LIFE was like that and even more so over the weekend. A surprising number of people turned up for the private view and party afterwards and luckily for Aunt Patsy and me most of them solved the sleeping problem by staying up all night singing. Richard played the piano which was lovely and Donald the Minibus played the bagpipes which was excruciating. I only like the sound of bagpipes at a distance of several miles.

I organized a squad of people to make sandwiches and fry eggs until I nearly fell asleep over the kitchen table where Aunt Patsy found me and sent me off to bed. I was so tired that not even the roar of voices, the singing and the pipes, could keep me awake for more than two minutes.

The next day we took it in turns to guard the gallery while the others slept. Richard and I escorted the visitors who were returning to the Mainland to catch the morning boat from the jetty. (Everyone on Stranday spoke about the Mainland as if Oban, Glasgow, Edinburgh and London were equally foreign and far away and we were beginning to do so too.)

When we got to the gallery after dawdling along the shore, we found Aunt Patsy talking to a thin grey-haired man and his stout, equally grey-haired wife.

'Emma,' she said, 'this is Mr Kilpatrick, the headmaster of the school. I've just been telling him about you.'

I shook hands with them both, rather amazed that Aunt Patsy could bring herself to speak to any headmaster except in the strict line of duty, but as they went on talking I realized why. They were what Aunt Patsy and Stephen called 'civilized'. Mr Kilpatrick was a keen naturalist, he had collections of birds' eggs, butterflies and moths. Mrs Kilpatrick kept bees and promised us some honey. They both knew about archaeology and geology and spoke of walking along the beach with little hammers, finding moss agates and amethysts which Mr Kilpatrick cut and polished in his workshop.

He was very keen on his school doing projects of one sort and another and agreed that examinations were the bane of education.

'You see, Emma,' said Aunt Patsy triumphantly.

'But I have to pass my O-levels,' I murmured sullenly.

At this, Mr Kilpatrick changed his tactics and while Aunt

Patsy wandered off with Mrs Kilpatrick, probably to find out if they believed in eating seaweed and nettles, he started questioning me about my schoolwork.

'So you are due to take O-levels in March?' he asked. 'What subjects?'

'English, French, History, Geography, Maths and Latin,' I said.

'An impressive list. Do you have any favourite subjects?'

'History, mostly.'

'That's spendid. You might be interested to help me with research for the history of Stranday I'm working on now.'

'I might,' I said cautiously.

'And I understand Glasgow University is sponsoring a dig some time in the near future. My son, Douglas, applied to join the team when some of them were prospecting the site at Easter.'

'A dig?' I queried.

'An archaeological excavation. I expect they'll measure up this summer and start work next. I'm looking forward to that as I've done a certain amount of research on my own. Interested?'

'I might be.' I did not want to make firm plans until we were absolutely settled and I had got my O-levels out of the way.

'Any idea of how you want to earn your living?' he went on. 'I was going to say "what you want to be" but that's a ridiculous way of putting it. You can be what you want, regardless, but you may need to earn your living as well.'

' I haven't got as far as that,' I mumbled, 'but I had thought something to do with research.'

'We'll have a long talk before term begins,' said Mr Kilpatrick. Then he changed the subject and began telling me about the school.

'It's only a small one, sixty-three pupils at the moment. Miss Davidson takes the babies, Mrs McGrath the eight-to-elevens and I take the rest. There are advantages and disadvantages. It means that you have to work on your own a good deal but it also means there is no one to hold you back.

It means that we don't have a lot of fancy equipment but it does mean we can cater for individual tastes. There are about half a dozen people taking O-levels, I think, and since the powers-that-be consider it to be a necessary examination, of course we pay some attention to it.'

'What happens after that?'

'Oh, you have to go to the Mainland, to Oban High School. There are special hostels but you can get home for long weekends and holidays. Of course, there ought to be a proper secondary school on the island or at least an annexe . . .'

But I was not listening. 'Hostels!' I said, bristling. The idea of staying in a hostel when I had just started enjoying life in our cottage filled me with horror.

'Oh don't worry, Emma, it may never happen,' said Richard impatiently when I confided in him.

'What do you mean?'

'You may be sick of living here by then.'

'I'm quite sure I won't.'

Now we had settled in I could not imagine living anywhere else and I often forgot that we only had the cottage for five years. Brain drain or not, I hoped Stephen's friend would stay in America for ever. Richard appeared to enjoy our new life too; he swam, climbed, fished and walked and I was quite offended when, after a fortnight, he said he was leaving.

'I thought you liked it here,' I said, disappointed.

'My dear Emma, of course I like it. But I have to do some work before term starts.'

'There's a piano here,' I muttered.

'If I play the piano I'm bound to be interrupted by some gawping tourist asking stupid questions. This is a marvellous holiday place but I've had my holiday now.'

No one can argue with Richard so I just had to resign myself. He set off for Edinburgh to prepare for his first University term; I began school; Aunt Patsy and Stephen closed the gallery and concentrated on their work; we cleared the civilized room for use at weekends or whenever anyone had time or energy to light a fire.

Apart from people arriving unexpectedly for the weekend with consequent food crises, the time a violent storm prevented the steamer calling and we were without bread for several days, and various other alarms, life settled down and we began to feel we had been living on the island all our lives. People accepted us and we accepted them.

Our nearest neighbour was an old lady of eighty-two who supplied us with eggs and milk. I thought at first she was a witch. She had white, angry-looking hair, a huge nose with a wart on it, a shawl over her head, long black skirts and black woollen stockings. When Aunt Patsy and I went to collect the milk, wearing shorts, she made pointed remarks about 'young folks going round half-naked nowadays – and the old ones too.' Another time when she met us in the pouring rain and Aunt Patsy made some comment on the dreadful weather, she croaked: 'We're lucky that it's not raining fire and brimstone.'

This convulsed us and we hurried home to tell Stephen. For ever afterwards when anything disastrous occurred we said solemnly, 'We're lucky it's not fire and brimstone.'

Donald the Minibus was a big brawny man, who worked a croft in his spare time. He was a fierce Scottish Nationalist – I rather think he wanted self-government for Stranday as well – played the pipes, got drunk at the Ardloch Hotel every Saturday and had three daughters, all very beautiful and intelligent.

Hamish was red-haired, young and rather sad. He had wanted to marry the girl who worked in the Ardloch Hotel but she was a Protestant and he was a Catholic (the island was pretty well divided between the two religions) and the parents, the Minister and the priest all objected. He owned the boat we had arrived on, taking tourist trips here and there during the summer, and in between he worked a croft and went fishing. He was given to arriving at our cottage rather late in the evening, in a melancholy mood, prepared to sing sad Gaelic folk songs with eighty-four verses.

Dougal, his friend, was as swarthy as a gipsy, with high cheekbones and straight black hair. He lived with his old mother and if he was ever out late at a party she would arrive in her nightgown, an old coat hung over her shoulders, and drag him home.

The Kilpatricks became our closest friends. Aunt Patsy and Stephen called them Michael and Dorothy but as I was still at school I stuck to Mr and Mrs. I liked Mr Kilpatrick but he had a tendency so many teachers have, of handing out great slabs of information all the time. This was all very well at school but in his home or ours I did not like being made to feel that I ought to whip out a jotter to make notes or to say at intervals: 'Yes, sir.' Mrs Kilpatrick was always fussing over her bees or emerging dishevelled from the kitchen where she had been baking bread, brewing wine or making jam and chutney.

Their son Douglas was also studying for his O-levels and though he was miserably shy at first we gradually became friends. He had dark untidy hair, a gap between his two front teeth and was always falling over or upsetting things, blushing furiously. He had a stammer and used to say: 'Sh-sh-shall we go to the c-c-c-cinema, Emma?' (There was a small hall in Ardloch where very old films were shown once a week.) He wanted to become a film director, and used to embarrass me at the cinema by talking – he did not stammer in the dark – learnedly about panning and long shots and filters.

I also liked a girl in my class called Christine whose ambition was to leave the island and become a typist in an office on the Mainland – Oban, Glasgow or London, I never discovered which. She was never tired of listening to my descriptions of shops, buses, coffee bars and cinemas, which made me feel worldly and sophisticated.

Every morning I went to collect the milk while Stephen or Aunt Patsy prepared breakfast and then the minibus called to take me to school. When I came home I would inspect their work in the gallery and then we would all have tea together. In the evenings we talked, read, listened to records and I did my homework.

Against this routine were the little excitements: fishing, going to the cinema, eating Saturday lunch at the hotel, visiting the Kilpatricks, Aunt Patsy selling a new design,

Stephen finishing a picture. But these excitements were as much a part of our routine as the scarlet hips on the brown autumn hedges.

So it was almost like a revolution when, one evening, Aunt Patsy said dreamily, looking into the fire: 'I'm going to have a baby, Emma.'

I felt so stunned I couldn't think of anything to reply except: 'When?'

'March, I think. Isn't it marvellous?'

'Mmm.'

She smiled idiotically and Stephen, on the other side of the fire, put his hand on hers and they gazed blissfully into each other's eyes.

I knew I ought to jump up and make all sorts of congratulatory remarks but I couldn't. All I could at first think of was that they had had this secret between them and not told me; that it would be their own baby while I was merely adopted; that I would be left out of the warm family circle and our pleasant life would be disrupted.

I did have enough sense to know that I must not say any of this so I tried to summon up the old Emma who bullied them about washing-up and regular meal-times.

'So long as it's in the school holidays,' I said gruffly, 'I'll be prepared to help.'

Chapter Five

For the next few days I did not actually sulk but when I joined in the conversation my voice sounded peculiar because my throat was so hot and tight. Though I did my share of the chores as usual I never volunteered to do anything extra and I spent most of my free time reading on my bed or going for long walks along the shore.

Inside me there were two Emmas who argued interminably.

Emma 1. Now pull yourself together. Married people always want babies of their own.

Emma 2. But they'll love it more than me.

Emma 1. Why shouldn't they? The way you're behaving now no one can love you.

Emma 2. Babies are disgusting, they smell of sick and wet nappies and they're always yelling.

Emma 1. Nonsense. Babies are lovely and cuddly. It will be just like having a little sister.

Emma 2. Who wants a sister fifteen years younger? I shall have to stay at home with it while Aunt Patsy and Stephen go out and enjoy themselves. It will spoil everything.

Emma 1. You ought to be jolly glad to be able to help them after all they've done for you.

Emma 2. Pooh! Gratitude! I work as hard as any au pair girl.

Emma 1. And why not? If it wasn't for Aunt Patsy you'd be in a home or a ghastly boarding school or living with Aunt Laura.

Emma 2. They should have asked me how I felt about it beforehand.

Emma 1. Don't be so absurd. It's their business. You're just suffering from common or garden jealousy. And that's disgusting.

Emma 2. If only my parents hadn't died I wouldn't have had to be adopted at all.

Emma 1. (beginning again) Now pull yourself together.

The longer these arguments went on, the more silent and gloomy I became. When Aunt Patsy or Stephen asked me if I wasn't feeling well or if something at school was worrying me I bit their heads off. 'I'm perfectly all right, thank you, for goodness sake leave me alone.'

'I think we ought to make an expedition to the north of the island and see this nature conservancy place,' Stephen said one Saturday evening. 'There's a boat going tomorrow, Hamish says, for the Minister, who takes a service there once a month. What about it, Emma?'

'I don't mind,' I said languidly.

'What about you, Patsy?'

'I'd be sick if I looked at a boat,' said Aunt Patsy ruefully, 'besides I've got to get some designs ready for Monday's steamer.'

'All right. Emma and I will go. Do you think you could rustle up some sandwiches, Emma?'

'I suppose so.'

If Stephen had said, 'Well, jolly well stay at home and sulk, I'll get the sandwiches myself,' I could hardly have blamed him, but he didn't. He looked at me thoughtfully, merely saying:

'Remember to put on warm clothes. It's likely to be pretty chilly in an open boat.'

I could not face his look of kind concern. If I had I would have burst into tears and confessed my horrid, jealous thoughts. Instead I mumbled goodnight and retired to bed.

The next morning we rode down to the jetty, stacked our bikes in the shed and waited for Hamish to arrive from Coll, with the Minister and a couple of women visiting relations on Stranday.

It was a lovely clear September day and it was impossible not to enjoy spinning over the bouncing waves. The trees were yellow or that coppery sort of green they always go at the beginning of autumn; the heather on the hills was blackish-purple; the bracken a foxy brown. The sun glinted the waves, cutting out diamonds of light that made my eyes ache.

Hamish steered the boat close to the shore to get the protection of the cliffs and as we passed our cottage we could see Aunt Patsy waving. Then we rounded the south-west tip of the island and sailed up the far side where I had never been before.

Stephen was talking to Hamish but the noise of the outboard motor drowned what they were saying so I just stared at the sea and the sky, the high cliffs and wheeling gulls. The Minister, in a silent hump, was obviously concentrating on his sermon.

At last we reached a small bay where the nature conservancy people lived in a dozen or so houses scattered on the level ground. The arms of the bay were steep and rocky but at the far end a small river flowed into the sea from a long wooded valley.

Hamish tied up the boat to an iron ring at the quay and we all climbed up the stone steps, stretching our legs and blinking as you always do when you get off a boat or out of a car.

The Minister was met by some ladies in hats and gloves who walked off with him to a small wooden hall where the service was going to be held. Hamish started tinkering with his boat and told Stephen and me to come back in a couple of hours' time.

First we called at the Warden's house. The Warden, a Scoutmasterish type of man, took us round, answering all Stephen's questions.

He told us that they were trying to make the island as fertile as it had been in the time before the Clearances when the people had been forced to emigrate to make way for sheep. Now they were planting trees and clearing bracken; breeding deer and ponies; they had a model farm with pigs, cows and sheep; each year they increased their arable land; they made their own electricity; also they were encouraging the wild life, birds and badgers and so on, to restore the natural balance. There were about two dozen families living there at present with a small school for the five-and six-year-olds who were too little to go all the way to Ardloch.

Stephen was fascinated by all this and began in turn to tell the Warden his plans for the gallery. They both became quite excited.

'Of course what we need is a proper harbour,' said the Warden. 'At the moment only small craft can call and in bad weather . . .' he shrugged his shoulders.

'What's the road like?' asked Stephen.

'It needs re-surfacing,' the Warden answered dryly.

By this time I was getting bored so I said I thought I would take a walk.

'Meet me at the jetty at half past twelve and we'll eat our sandwiches,' said Stephen, 'and now,' turning to the Warden, 'tell me . . .'

I set off up a path along the bank of the river, a lovely brown river that leapt over big grey stones. The ground was carpeted with springy mountain turf, starred with little bright-coloured flowers. On the other side of the river some ponies were grazing in a field and beyond that a hillside rose steeply, covered with baby fir trees.

Ahead lay a dark pine forest fringed with delicate golden birch trees. It was all very peaceful and I think I would have thrown off my bad mood if Stephen had been waiting at the jetty when I returned. But there was no sign of him and suddenly I felt aggrieved and resentful all over again.

'He doesn't care a fig about me,' I muttered, kicking a stone into the sea. 'Well, when he does come back I won't be here either.'

I began to climb up a steep rocky path, which led through some twisted thorn bushes, on to a series of rocky hills, bare except for patches of turf or heather.

I climbed up and up, holding on to rocks and heather, until I was panting and had to stop for breath. I looked back the way I had come and suddenly there was nothing between me and the sea foaming angrily far below. I shut my eyes, my legs collapsed and I sprawled over the rock, my heart beating furiously, sweat pouring down my face, my breath coming in sharp little sobs.

However was I going to get down again? I simply did not dare to move.

The words came into my head: 'It will serve them right,' and then instantly I was ashamed.

At last, very gradually, I began to move my feet downwards from one rocky ledge to another, sobbing all the time and mumbling half under my breath, 'Please help me, oh please help me, oh please.' I did not dare to look down again in case the sight of that terrible sea would send me plummeting into it like a gannet. Then, just as I was almost within reach of the first thorn tree, the rock under one foot gave way and went careering down the slope and I was so terrified that I screamed: 'Stephen! Help!' and shut my eyes again.

I must have fainted because the next thing I heard were

voices and footsteps and Stephen saying in an agitated voice: 'She's here. Emma! Are you hurt?' And he was sitting beside me and gently turning me over.

'N-no,' I whispered, clutching him.

He hoisted me to my feet and then with him and the Warden holding me tightly on either side, we began very slowly to descend.

The way down was not really dangerous and steep. It had been the sudden view of the sea that had upset me. So I began to feel dreadfully ashamed, especially when the Warden insisted upon me going into his house to lie down and drink a cup of sweet tea.

'A nasty attack of vertigo,' he said capably. 'Didn't you know you had no head for heights?'

I shook my head.

'You're never to do that sort of thing again,' said Stephen angrily.

'I'm sorry.'

'So you jolly well ought to be. Think what Patsy would have felt if you arrived home on a stretcher.'

I hated him for being so angry and myself for having been so stupid.

On the boat he wrapped me in a rug and sat beside me while this time the Minister, having no sermon to plan, talked to Hamish.

'Emma,' Stephen said. He did not sound angry any more.

'Yes.'

'Did you really not know you were afraid of heights?'

'I – I don't know.'

'Hmmm,' he looked at me questioningly but I did not meet his gaze. 'Look,' he continued, 'you're not happy about the baby, are you? I wish you were. It's upsetting Patsy. We both thought you'd like it, having a sister, a cousin, I mean.'

I began to cry. I couldn't help it. Not noisy crying, fortunately, but several tears bubbled out of my eyes and trickled down my face. I sniffed and Stephen passed me his handkerchief.

'Talk to me, Emma,' he said, 'tell me what you feel, don't bottle it up.'

I shook my head. There was nothing to say. I had no intention of revealing my ignoble thoughts.

'Do you miss your parents?' Stephen asked.

'Sometimes.'

It was just two years ago since they had died. When I was happy I didn't miss them but when I was worried or miserable, I did.

'I can't say that Patsy and I feel like parents towards you because I don't know how parents feel – yet,' said Stephen, 'but we feel you belong with us and always will, even if we have ten more children, which is extremely unlikely.' He grinned. 'One baby will probably drive me up the wall.'

I wiped my face with his handkerchief and smiled back.

'I don't suppose Patsy will know which end is which. You know we rely on you for so many things. I sometimes feel it's unfair.'

'It's not unfair. I like it.'

'Good.' And then he began to talk about the nature conservancy place and the Minister joined in, telling us about the history of Stranday and describing what it had been like in the olden days before the Clearances.

'It could be like that again,' he said, 'and even better because of electricity and modern farming methods.'

I sat feeling warm and weak beside them, not saying much, until we reached our own side of the island and anchored at the jetty.

'Do you think you can cope with the ride home?' Stephen asked solicitously.

'Of course,' I said indignantly, jumping on to my bike. 'I'll race you if you like.'

'Certainly not. I'm too old. What's the betting that Patsy has forgotten the time and that there is no delicious meal waiting for us?'

'Ten to one,' I replied. 'Stephen, don't tell her about my – accident. She might be worried.'

'We'd both get a row,' said Stephen. 'Lord, I'm hungry!'

'Perhaps there'll be nettles,' I said saucily.

Chapter Six

'WHO's having this baby, you or Patsy?' asked Richard furiously. It was the evening of Christmas Day and we were having almost the first quarrel in our lives.

After my talk with Stephen in the boat I had turned over a new leaf with a vengeance and appointed myself as Aunt Patsy's guardian. I read her books on how to have and look after a baby until I could have passed exams on the subject. One of the books was about exercises and relaxation and I drilled her remorselessly so that Stephen was always finding her in some curious position on the floor while I, with the book of instructions in one hand, called out: 'One, two, blow! One, two, blow!'

'And you've got to drink a pint of milk a day,' I told her severely.

'Ugh, horrible stuff.'

I did not trust her so I made a point of bringing her a glassful in the middle of the morning when she was working in the gallery and another just before I went to bed. What is more, I stayed with her until she had drunk it.

After lunch I insisted upon her lying down for an hour.

'But I'm not tired, Emma,' Aunt Patsy would say plaintively, 'and I've so much work to do.'

'And no smoking,' I pointed out nastily.

I accompanied her to Oban with a list of baby clothes and equipment down to the last safety-pin and supervised all her purchases.

I copied out the telephone numbers of the doctor and the midwife and every night before I went to bed I checked my bicycle so that I would be able to scorch down to the telephone at Ardloch at a moment's notice.

'We really ought to have a telephone of our own,' I told Stephen.

'I know, love, but we can't afford it at the moment.'

Stephen was rather amused by my tyranny though now and again he protested:

'Don't fuss, Emma. Patsy's in the best of health. She'll have the baby as easily as a cat has kittens.'

We agreed that if the baby was a boy he should be called Mark but if it was a girl Aunt Patsy wanted to call her Lucy.

'Lucy!' I screamed, 'if you call her Lucy I'll never speak to you again.'

So we compromised on Vanessa.

I was so intoxicated by the idea of being in charge that I did not realize how tiresome my bullying must have been because Aunt Patsy, although in her thirties, was young and strong, had never been ill in her life, and both the doctor and the midwife assured us that there were no likely complications. She never had morning sickness, she walked, bicycled and gardened as usual; worked half the night if she felt inclined (she was doing some really gorgeous designs for dress material at the moment); and she would have continued lifting heavy paraffin cans and buckets of coal if I had not strictly forbidden it.

But if my attitude amused Aunt Patsy and Stephen, it did not amuse Richard at all. At first, when he came to stay over Christmas week, he watched and listened with a rather puzzled expression on his face. But after Christmas dinner, when we were sitting in the civilized room listening to records, Aunt Patsy held out her glass for Stephen to refill with wine.

'No,' I said firmly, 'one glass is enough. I'll fetch you some milk.'

'Oh shut up, Emma,' said Richard gruffly.

'It's Christmas,' pleaded Aunt Patsy. 'Wine can't hurt.'

'The book says an occasional glass and you've had one.'

It was at this point that Richard burst out:

'Who's having the baby, you or Patsy?' (He had gradually stopped calling her 'Aunt' but I could never remember to do the same.)

'I sometimes wonder,' said Stephen treacherously.

'I'm only trying to help,' I retorted.

'You're a tremendous help,' said Aunt Patsy feebly, 'but—'

'But!' Richard exploded. 'But she's a bossy, tyrannical, domineering, interfering little slob.'

He got up, took the wine bottle and ostentatiously filled Aunt Patsy's glass.

'You,' I hurled back at him 'are an ignorant, insensitive, moronic barbarian!'

'Children!' expostulated Aunt Patsy.

'Now, now!' feebly added Stephen.

I glared at them all and rushed out of the room. So this was all the thanks I got for cherishing my aunt.

Later, Richard knocked on my door but I shouted: 'Go away!'

I was still huffy the next day at breakfast but I graciously consented to go for a walk with Richard so that we could continue our quarrel in private. In the bitter cold our words did not have the same edge. After we had flung a few choice epithets at each other, he began in a different tone of voice:

'Listen, Emma, you've got to stop this nonsense.'

I scowled. 'I don't know what you mean.'

'I come here and find you absolutely obsessed by this wretched baby. You've hardly asked me how I'm getting on with my music; you haven't wanted me to play to you; you haven't told me anything about yourself. All you want to do is to talk about babies. And you bully Patsy disgracefully.'

'Someone has to be firm with her,' I muttered.

'That someone doesn't have to be you.'

We were walking along the beach, occasionally skiffing stones, and now I did a beauty. 'Look, Richard, a sixer.'

'Well done. But don't change the subject.'

'You're a bully too.'

'Someone has to be firm with you and that person does have to be me.'

One of the things about people with red hair – and Richard and I both have red hair – is that you can be furious one minute and perfectly equable the next.

We skiffed a few more pebbles and then began to look for driftwood along the tide line.

'Tell me about school,' Richard said companionably.

'It's not bad. Mr Kilpatrick's teaching some of us geology. And there are going to be archaeologists here next summer, digging for something. Mr Kilpatrick says they'll need volunteers as well as students – I might do that.'

'Sounds interesting. Are you going to get your O-levels all right?'

'I expect so. Exams are stupid.'

'They may be but it doesn't stop us having to pass them.'

To tell the truth I had been changing my mind about the value of education. Life on the island was so pleasant and absorbing that it had just been faintly crossing my mind that I'd leave at the end of the year and not bother about pursuing an academic career. But I did not want to risk another quarrel with Richard.

'How's your music?' I asked, changing the subject.

'I'll play you my new piece when we get back. But Emma, I'm serious, don't mug your exams because you're so absorbed in baby management. You know I think Patsy and Stephen are fabulous characters but don't let them swamp you and don't try to live their lives for them. You've got to be yourself and live your own.'

'Oh brother, what big words you use.'

'All the better to knock some sense into you.'

I took a swipe at him and he started running. I chased him, though naturally without catching him, and when we reached home we were friends again.

Although I would not have dreamed of admitting it to him, I did have a little twinge of guilt about my school work. Mr Kilpatrick was a splendid teacher if you were keen, but he was not specially firm about homework being done and if I said I understood something he believed me and did not bother to find out if I really did. He tended to regard O-levels as a disagreeable necessity and I remembered the disagreeable part and forgot the necessity. Still, when term started again he decided to hold mock exams so that he could see what each of us ought to concentrate on until the real ones. They were much more difficult than I had imagined.

In fact I only passed English and History. He gave us our marks separately in his own room and after showing me mine he looked at me in a puzzled way.

'What happened, Emma?' he asked.

'I don't know,' I muttered, hot with embarrassment.

'At some schools you simply would not be allowed to sit Latin and Geography – on the basis of these marks.'

'I know.'

'However, I refuse to believe that they bear any relation to what you could do if you tried. I know you have been pretty busy helping your uncle and aunt but now you must put your own work first. Do you want me to have a chat with them?'

'No,' I almost shouted. 'Please no.'

'All right. But remember, Emma, apply yourself for the next three months and if you need any help I'm here to give it.'

I mumbled my thanks and then, bitterly ashamed, I crawled home and hid in my bedroom.

I lay on my bed, staring at the ceiling and saying: 'Who cares? Stupid old exams!' to comfort myself, but I knew at the bottom of my heart that for a person like me, without any special talents, they were important. For an awful moment I imagined how upset my mother and father would have been.

Aunt Patsy came up and asked me if I was all right.

'Headache,' I lied. She fetched me a cup of tea and two aspirin.

'How was school?' she asked, sitting down beside me on the bed.

'Awful. Mr Kilpatrick gave me a row.'

'Do you want Stephen to go and knock him down?'

'No, no, he's all right.' I said hastily, though I was tempted to let Aunt Patsy think that he was to blame. 'You see, it's just – I failed some of my exams.'

'You failed?' said Aunt Patsy in amazement. 'Stephen shall certainly knock Mr Kilpatrick down. It's absolutely ridiculous. He told me you were one of the brightest girls he's ever taught. Stephen!' she called, dashing out of the room.

I scrambled off the bed and pursued her down to the kitchen where Stephen was drinking tea.

'Another moronic schoolmaster,' she began but I interrupted.

'No, it wasn't his fault. It was mine.' I took a deep breath. 'I've been lazy. I've been skipping my homework. I deserved to fail.'

It was a difficult thing to say but the moment I had admitted it I felt better.

'Anyhow, it doesn't matter. You know what I think of this conveyor-belt education,' Aunt Patsy went on, still bubbling with indignation, but Stephen stopped her.

'Quiet, Patsy,' he said, and he *could* be firm when he wanted. Then he began asking me exactly what I had done and had not done.

'Emma, you and Patsy may be in charge of the baby front,' he said at last, 'but I am in charge of the education front. From now on you will report to me for homework duty every night and you shall not rise from your desk until it has all been done – to my satisfaction. Agreed?'

'Dictator!' snorted Aunt Patsy.

But I agreed. Sometimes it is very restful to be taken charge of.

Chapter Seven

WHEN the baby started it was not at all as I had imagined. I had set my heart on a dramatic ride at two o'clock in the morning, preferably in a gale or a snowstorm, but what really happened was that Stephen knocked on my door at seven and told me that breakfast was ready. 'We think the baby's started,' he added, almost as an afterthought. I dressed like lightning, and almost fell downstairs to find them both sitting quietly, eating scrambled eggs and drinking coffee.

'How are you? Are you all right? Shall I go for the midwife?'

'Sit down and have your breakfast,' said Aunt Patsy smiling, 'there's lots of time.'

She looked just as usual, though a little flushed and excited. Every ten minutes or so she leaned forward with closed eyes, breathing slowly just as the book had told her to do. Stephen held her hand across the table and each time she opened her eyes again, he said: 'You're marvellous!' or 'Well done, darling.'

'Does it hurt?' I asked anxiously.

'No, but it's a most peculiar feeling,' replied Aunt Patsy.

After breakfast they insisted on the chores being done as usual. Aunt Patsy washed up, I dried, Stephen got in the wood and the coal.

'This is a fine time to begin being methodical,' I groaned. I was nearly mad with impatience before they told me I could go to ring the midwife.

It was a blowy day but luckily the wind was behind me so I positively swooped into Ardloch like a bird.

Although I knew perfectly well that having babies nowadays was nothing to make a fuss about, I could not help being influenced by the novels I had read in which the mortality of mothers and babies must have been considerably higher than in real life. Now I remembered all the descriptions of sweat and groans and struggles and yells, with the expectant father striding up and down, pulling his hair out in handfuls, and the midwife and doctor padding up and downstairs, with set grim faces and kettles of boiling water.

I suppose once you have experienced the death of people you love, you never quite recapture your confidence. If anything went wrong with Aunt Patsy there was no hospital on the island, only a helicopter ambulance that whisked emergency patients to the Mainland. And that might take too long.

So my hand was trembling when I dialled the midwife's number and my voice came out in a breathless squeak.

'It's Aunt Patsy,' I said, 'I mean, Mrs McTaggart. The baby's started.'

45

The midwife, whose name was Mrs Cameron, had a nice friendly Glasgow voice.

'I'll be round in half an hour,' she assured me. 'Is your aunt fine?'

'Oh yes. She's doing her breathing beautifully.'

'Now don't you worry, my lassie, everything will go fine, just you see. I'll give the doctor a ring before he starts out on his round.'

'You will hurry, won't you?'

'Aye, I'll hurry. You go home and put the kettle on. We'll need lots of cups of tea.'

The ride home took twice as long because the wind now blew straight into my face and buffeted the bike all over the road so that I had to dismount and walk part of the way. By the time I got home Mrs Cameron, who had a scooter, had already arrived and they were all sitting in the kitchen having tea. Surely it was about time something more exciting happened?

But they just sat chatting about the weather and island affairs. At last Mrs Cameron stood up and said:

'Well, dearie, time to go to work,' and she and Aunt Patsy walked slowly upstairs.

'You and I, Emma,' Stephen said, 'had better find something useful to do. What are we going to have for lunch?'

'Lunch?'

'We have to keep our strength up. Better make something complicated that will take a long time.'

'There's chops,' I said.

'Well, turn them into an Irish stew so that we can eat it any time – and cut the potatoes wafer-thin. First I shall shave so that I shall be worthy of the honour of fatherhood.'

So Stephen shaved and I made the stew; then he went outside to saw logs while I did the ironing; then he cleaned the windows while I polished the floor; then he wrote some business letters while I knitted a jersey for Mark or Vanessa.

We both jumped a couple of feet into the air when Mrs Cameron called down:

'Would you bring us up some more tea, if you please.'

We both dived for the teapot, nearly bumping our heads, so that we began to giggle and the milk got spilt.

'This will never do,' said Stephen.

Upstairs the room already smelt hospitally. Aunt Patsy was lying propped up by her pillows and Mrs Cameron was sitting beside her, knitting.

'Everything's just grand,' she said cheerfully.

'Come and talk to me,' said Aunt Patsy. 'I need entertaining. What have you two been doing downstairs?'

'We've practically spring-cleaned the house,' said Stephen, 'or we will have if this goes on much longer.'

'You know what I thought,' said Aunt Patsy, and then she closed her eyes, breathing deeply. 'I thought,' she went on, 'we ought to learn weaving. People are crazy about hand-woven stuff. We could do rugs and shawls.'

'Splendid,' said Stephen uneasily.

'We'll use the traditional colours and make up our own designs.'

'Why not?' said Stephen. 'Back to cottage industry.'

'You don't sound very enthusiastic.'

'My mind,' said Stephen, 'is on other things.'

Aunt Patsy laughed.

'Go downstairs and have a stiff whisky,' she said, 'I don't mind.'

'He's bearing up fine,' said Mrs Cameron. 'Often the men are more trouble than the women.'

Stephen kissed Aunt Patsy, saying: 'I'll be up again presently.'

'And you, Emma,' said Aunt Patsy, 'put something on the record-player, something noisy so that I can hear it. Beethoven perhaps.'

So Stephen and I lit the fire in the civilized room. He drank some whisky and I played records and knitted, until Mrs Cameron called again and asked if it was time for dinner.

There was nothing I wanted less but I dished out some of the stew. Stephen took Aunt Patsy's upstairs and sat with her while Mrs Cameron ate hers with me in the kitchen.

'You're a right good cook,' she said approvingly, shovelling great forkfuls into her mouth. 'Some folk can only manage a boiled egg on occasions like this. And how do you like life on the island?'

'It's marvellous,' I said, chewing a bit of potato at least two hundred times before I could swallow it.

'I used to work in a big hospital in Glasgow, all rush and hurry, no time to get to know my mothers at all. I've been here ten years now and never lost a baby or a mother. Ah, do I hear the doctor's car?'

Dr Ogilvie was red-faced and cheerful. He always travelled with his big golden retriever beside him in the car and spent most of his time fishing because so few people were ever ill.

'Good morning, Mrs Cameron, how are things going? Hello, Emma. Not at school? Now if I can just wash my hands . . .'

As if I would go to school on a day like this! I stared at his back contemptuously as he and Mrs Cameron went upstairs together. Then Stephen came down with Aunt Patsy's empty plate and his own nearly full one.

'It was delicious, Emma,' he apologized, 'but somehow I'm not particularly hungry. Keep it in the oven. Maybe we'll feel more peckish later.'

Now we gave up any attempt to keep busy, we just sat staring at each other, straining our ears for what was going on upstairs.

'It's all more difficult than I supposed,' said Stephen ruefully. 'Patsy's marvellous but you and I, Emma, are not marvellous at all.'

'I know.'

'Do you think it would be bestial of me to have some more whisky?'

He was just pouring it out when we heard a cry, a completely different voice from Aunt Patsy's, a shrill baby voice.

'It's born,' almost shouted Stephen and he hugged me tightly as we listened again.

'I'm going to her,' and he bounded up the stairs, two at a time. I followed more slowly, my heart hammering with excitement.

48

Aunt Patsy was lying, not pale and wan and exhausted as she would have been in a novel, but flushed and dishevelled as if she had been for a long walk in the wind. 'Oh darlings,' she murmured joyfully. 'Look!'

Mrs Cameron was wrapping in a blanket a small creature with a red face and a mop of dark hair.

'It's a lassie,' she said proudly, 'a fine wee lassie.'

Stephen sat down beside the bed and took Aunt Patsy's hand and kissed her, murmuring undistinguishable words. I tiptoed to the other side of the bed and kissed her too. I was feeling quite choked up with excitement, happiness and relief.

Half an hour later when Aunt Patsy had been cleaned up and the baby had been washed and dressed, Stephen suddenly cried:

'Surprise! I'd completely forgotten.' He'd had a bottle of champagne keeping cool in a bucket of water to celebrate. Now he brought it up and we all sat round Aunt Patsy's bed to drink it, wishing health, wealth, happiness, beauty, talent and a long life for Vanessa.

Then Aunt Patsy settled down for a sleep; the doctor drove away in his car; Mrs Cameron puttered off on her scooter and Stephen and I were left alone.

'Who shall we tell, Emma? Shall you or I go down to Ardloch to spread the glad news?'

He need not have worried. News travels so fast on an island that people often know it before it has happened. All afternoon and evening people kept arriving with honey and eggs, early daffodils and whisky, baby clothes and chocolates, congratulating Stephen and asking tenderly after Aunt Patsy and Vanessa.

In between visitors, Stephen and I tiptoed upstairs to see that they were both all right.

About nine o'clock Aunt Patsy woke up, ravenously hungry, but unfortunately the stew had dried up. So I cooked her an enormous omelet using four eggs.

'I'm still hungry,' she complained when she had finished. 'Go and find me some bread and jam, Emma.'

Chapter Eight

'Emma, the Monster's crying. Do go and clonk her on the head,' demanded Aunt Patsy.

We were all in the gallery. I was learning to weave on a big hand-loom; Stephen was framing a new picture; Aunt Patsy was painting squiggles on some pottery plates; Vanessa, or the Monster as they called her, was outside in her pram yelling her head off.

'It's almost her bath-time,' I said, putting down the shuttle.

'Well, just amuse her for a minute until I finish this plate.'

I walked out into the May sunshine and scooped up Vanessa. She was usually a pretty baby with firm pink cheeks, Stephen's blue eyes and Aunt Patsy's dark hair, but at the moment, scarlet, tear-stained and crumpled, she did not look pretty at all.

I took her indoors, mopped her face, changed her nappy and brought her out again.

'Wuzzer, wuzzer,' I murmured comfortingly.

I dawdled round the garden showing Vanessa the trees, the birds and the grass and then stood idly at the door of the gallery, waiting for Aunt Patsy to finish. At last she looked up and sighed.

'Would you be an angel and bath her for me?' she coaxed.

Stephen looked up from his work and frowned.

'Patsy, for goodness sake, it's not Emma's job.'

'But Emma likes doing it, don't you, Emma?'

'I don't care what Emma likes. The fact remains that you're exploiting her.'

'Am I exploiting you, Emma?' Aunt Patsy asked lazily.

I did not reply to these rhetorical questions but just said:

'I'll bath her if you'll hold her for a minute while I get things ready.'

'I'll hold her,' said Stephen, wiping his hands on a turpentiney rag. 'Come to Daddy, Monster.'

He took her from me and nuzzled her neck.

'She's as fat as a butter ball,' he said admiringly.

Of course I was being exploited, for scenes like this happened every day.

'Emma, could you be an angel and bring the nappies in—' ... 'Emma, it's time for her orange juice—' ... 'Please would you—' ... 'Be a darling and—' ...

But I never – well, hardly ever – minded because quite literally there was nothing I wanted to do more. When I was little I had never played much with dolls and we had never had a dog or a cat so this was the first chance I had had to cuddle a warm, dependent, little creature. Whenever Vanessa looked at me with her periwinkle blue eyes, grinned at me showing her toothless gums, or clutched my hand with her small wiry fingers, my heart seemed to dissolve with tenderness. 'You're my baby,' I told her repeatedly.

Since I had passed my O-levels (except for Latin) Stephen had relaxed the homework rules and now I used to hurry home from school to play with Vanessa, wheel her out in her pram and more often than not give her her bath. School work, Mr Kilpatrick's projects, faded into insignificance compared with this fragile creature. Besides, I did not entirely trust Aunt Patsy. She might forget to dry and powder the ticklish places or drop her when she was slippery with soap. She might forget to sterilize the bottle we used for her orange juice.

Life with Vanessa had been pretty complicated and nerve-racking to start with since none of the three of us had had any first-hand experience with babies. Her crying and her silences seemed equally sinister.

'Do you think she is breathing?' we would whisper, hovering round her cot when she was asleep. Or, 'Perhaps the safety pin's come unfastened,' when she was crying. Moreover, Aunt Patsy now had more things to forget and more things to lose. She used to feed Vanessa anywhere she happened to be, so nappy-pins, talc powder and baby cream might be in the gallery or the kitchen or even, much to Stephen's disgust, in the civilized room. If I had not been there to bring some order into the establishment I do not know how they would have managed at all. But thanks to Dr Spock and Mrs Cameron I had become a wily and experienced baby-minder and there were few eventualities with which I could not cope.

Stephen was the only one who protested at my exploitation but he was working too hard to help with Vanessa himself. He hoped to get the gallery ready for its second opening in June, and when he was not working there he was in the garden planting potatoes, peas, beans and lettuces so that we should not have to eat nettles this summer.

Now and again I had a nagging feeling that I ought to be planning what to do with my life. Was I going to Oban High? Did I want to go to University? Did I really want a career, and if so what? But most of the time I did not think at all. I just enjoyed loving and looking after Vanessa; I was immersed in the rug I was weaving for the gallery opening; I helped Stephen in the garden; I occasionally remembered to write to Richard.

I think you have to live on an island to appreciate weather, there is so much of it and it seems to change every hour rather than every day. I never tired of watching the sea, pearly grey and flat like silk; wicked and green with great silver-maned breakers; bright blue, navy-blue, baby-blue. One moment the island would be drowned in white mist, colourless and damp. The next moment it would be glittering in the brightest of bright sunlight.

Into this happy vegetable existence Richard's letter seemed to come from a different country and a different century. He told me that an old school-friend of his had a car and that he wanted to make up a four and go, via Salzburg, to a music festival in Brno, Czechoslovakia.

'What about it?' Richard wrote. 'It won't cost much because we're camping. You'll only have to pay your share of the petrol and the grub. Bill is a good bloke and the other girl, Pauline, plays the oboe superbly. She is rather special, in fact I don't mind admitting that she and I are Going Steady, to use the vulgar parlance. I've written two sonatas for piano and oboe and when we perform together even the most hard-boiled critics faint with rapture and have to be hurried into the fresh air to be resuscitated. You must have been working quite hard, what with exams and the baby, so I'm sure Patsy and Stephen will think you deserve a proper holiday which you'll hardly get on that mad island. Please let me know soonest.'

Abroad – I'd never been abroad. Camping – I'd never been camping and though I imagined it might be rather uncomfortable, it would be fun too. Concerts – I had not been to a concert for ages. And there would be young, gay, intelligent people to talk to – my own generation.

But of course I could not go. How could I possibly leave Vanessa? And Aunt Patsy and Stephen were relying on me to help with the gallery during the summer. One of the problems of being adopted late in life is that you feel a sense of obligation, and the fact that I knew Aunt Patsy would say, 'Of course you must go,' made it impossible for me to ask. I knew Richard would just say that I was baby-fixated and that Patsy and Stephen must live their own lives and let me live mine but it was more complicated than that and I wished I had someone to discuss my problems with.

'What's the news from Richard?' Aunt Patsy asked as I thoughtfully put the letter away.

'Nothing much. He's met a girl called Pauline who plays the oboe.'

'Tell him to bring her here during the summer. There'll be room under the piano,' said Aunt Patsy enthusiastically. 'Would you be an angel and wash and dress Vanessa?'

I realize now that it is always unwise to be nobler than your character can stand. On this occasion the enormity of my sacrifice simply made me bad-tempered.

'Do you mind awfully if I don't?' I snapped. 'There are one or two things I must do.'

So I went up to my room to think things over. I would heroically tell Richard that funds were short and ask him to bring Pauline to Stranday instead. I would devote my summer to Vanessa and the gallery and suffer in silence.

I wrote the letter and intended to post it directly, before my nobility forsook me, but I discovered that we were out of envelopes. I would have to bike into Ardloch to buy some. It was at this moment that I realized that quite apart from my disappointment I felt decidedly peculiar. I was freezing cold. Half an hour later Aunt Patsy, coming in from the gallery to make some coffee, found me huddling over the fire wearing two winter jerseys.

'Emma, what on earth's the matter. It's not cold.'

'I think it's icy,' I replied, shivering.

'A brisk walk would be better than crouching over the fire!' she said sharply. Then she looked at me more closely and felt my forehead.

'I believe you've got a temperature.'

'But I can't have. I'm never ill.'

All the same I now noticed an aching sensation in my bones and my head felt stuffed with cotton-wool. I gazed blearily at Aunt Patsy.

'You're ill now. Trot off to bed and I'll bring you a hot water bottle.'

'But I can't go to bed. There isn't time. There's too much to do. How will you manage?' I babbled.

'Don't argue, Emma. Bed.'

I had never had any experience of being ill in Aunt Patsy's house but to my astonishment she did not turn a hair. She was up in a minute with a hot water bottle, a lemon drink and two aspirin.

'Stephen's just gone for Dr Ogilvie,' she said soothingly.

'Oh no,' I pleaded, 'not the doctor. I'll be all right in an hour or two, I promise.'

'Ssssh.'

'I want to finish weaving my rug before the gallery opens. And today's Saturday – I ought to bike down to the shop – Vanessa's out of cereal – I—'

'My dear Emma,' Aunt Patsy said affectionately, 'don't be such a little worrier. You may not believe it but I managed to look after myself for many years before you started looking after me.'

'I know, but – Vanessa—'

'Go to sleep.'

I lay back and thought how fed up she must be, having an invalid on her hands when there was so much to be done in the gallery. How could I have caught a germ in all this sea air?

According to Dr Ogilvie, however, I *had* caught a germ, some sort of flu, and if it didn't clear up in a few days he would put me on antibiotics. In the meantime I must stay in bed, keep warm, drink plenty of liquids and on no account must I see Vanessa in case of infection.

The next morning I woke up in a panic. I must get up and do my share of the Sunday chores regardless of Dr Ogilvie. But when I put a foot to the floor I felt sick and giddy and crawled back under the bedclothes.

I lay still and listened. I heard Vanessa's early morning noises, Aunt Patsy's voice telling her she was a monster, Stephen's bumble. Then I heard breakfast clatterings and presently Stephen came in and asked me how I felt.

'Like mud,' I moaned.

'Can I get you anything?'

'Perhaps a glass of lemonade. And could you fill my bottle.'

Stephen dexterously fished it out of the bottom of the bed.

'You poor old slob,' he said kindly and went downstairs whistling.

I had a horrible day. My temperature was just high enough for me to have no control over my thoughts which were more like dreams than thoughts, more like nightmares really.

I had sudden visions of Vanessa lying on the hearth-rug and a log falling out of the fire; of Vanessa upsetting her pram and being run over; of Vanessa smothering herself in her pillow. These far-fetched imaginings were followed by others, even more improbable: me cycling with Vanessa on the handlebars, taking her camping and finding I'd left the baby food behind, climbing up a mountain with Vanessa on my back and slipping down a gulley.

And although it is somehow wicked to imagine anyone

55

dead, I imagined Aunt Patsy and Stephen, being killed in a car smash like my own mother and father, leaving me to bring up Vanessa alone.

'Time for your temperature,' said Aunt Patsy, cheerily and very much alive, coming into my room.

'How's everything?' I murmured from a long way off.

'Everything's fine. The Monster has been almost an angel. I've finished my plates so I shall take a few days off.'

'Good,' I grunted through the thermometer, though in a way I was a little disappointed. There ought to have been a certain amount of chaos without me there to help.

Aunt Patsy held the thermometer up to the light and squinted at it.

'I can never read these wretched things,' she grumbled. 'Ah, wait a minute, I've got it. Oh dear, it's up to 102. Still, the doctor said he would be here around five and he'll give you something to bring it down.'

I made a protesting sound and she put her cool hand on my head, smoothed my hair back, straightened the pillow and smiled.

'Don't look so stricken, Emma,' she said, 'everyone gets ill some time. It's not a crime.'

Knowing that I had a temperature of 102 seemed to absolve me from responsibility. What did it matter who got the milk? What did it matter if meals were late? What did it matter if damp nappies and talc powder strayed round the house? If Vanessa went without her cereal for a couple of days? What did anything matter?

I felt as if I were floating. I stared at the curtains, which had designs of blue and green birds on a grey background, until the birds seemed to be flying. I stared at the ceiling until the lines and unevennesses became clouds and prehistoric monsters. When I was tired of staring I shut my eyes and listened. I listened to the swish and sigh of the sea, the rustle of leaves in the wind, the pattering of raindrops, until it all turned into Richard playing the piano and the seagulls' voices became Pauline on her oboe.

I dozed and floated and dozed again.

Chapter Nine

ON the very rare occasions in the past when I had been ill there had always been one particular day when I had felt well again, hungry and energetic and full of delight in ordinary things like walking in the garden, having a bath, feeling the wind in my hair and eating proper food. But this time I crawled downstairs still feeling like a mangy cat. Food disgusted me; Vanessa bored me; Aunt Patsy's vagaries exasperated me. I did not want to weave or garden or cycle or walk or read or cook. Some of the archaeologists had already arrived but though Mr Kilpatrick urged me to enrol as a volunteer, I could not be bothered.

I mooched round the house and garden, picking up things and putting them down again, grousing about the weather and the stove. If Aunt Patsy or Stephen asked me to do anything I sighed and said: 'Oh must I?' and if they made tender inquiries about my health I barked back: 'I feel perfectly all right. I'm just bored.'

I took to sitting on a rock in a sheltered part of the beach, staring gloomily out to sea, hating everyone, thinking long grumbling thoughts.

Nobody understood or appreciated me. I had given up my lovely holiday abroad for no reason at all since everyone could get along perfectly well without me. Nobody was interested in my problems. 'All they think about is their wretched gallery,' I thought. 'As if stupid pictures and pots and handwoven rugs are important. Vanessa doesn't care if I look after her or not. Nobody cares.'

I stopped trying to keep the cottage tidy; the sink was full of dirty dishes; the civilized room was littered with sketches, painting materials, baby clothes and coffee cups. I even neglected my own room, never making my bed or hanging up my clothes.

'The whole place is a pigsty but why should I bother?' I growled to myself.

The days crawled by and the gallery was almost ready for the opening in a week's time. If I had been in a pleasanter mood I would have appreciated what Stephen and Aunt Patsy had done – they had covered the walls in dark brown hessian, made beautiful display shelves for the pots and plates, and laid cream-coloured sisal matting on the bare cement floor.

'It looks even better than last year, doesn't it?' said Stephen as I inspected things with a jaundiced eye. 'But then we've had more time – and funds.' He and Aunt Patsy were busy with finishing touches while Vanessa, who hardly ever cried now, lay in her pram, clutching at the rays of sunlight that filtered through the beech tree.

'It's all right, I suppose,' I answered ungraciously.

'What on earth's got into you?' Stephen said, surprised and offended.

'Nothing.'

'Well, for goodness sake, you might at least be civil,' Aunt Patsy protested.

I could not bear the sight of their happiness so as usual I dawdled down to the shore to sit on my rock. It was not a particularly comfortable rock – what rock is? – but I did not want to be comfortable. I gazed out across the wide desolate sea. Could anything be more lonely than to be alone watching the waves pounding on the shingle? Could there be any noise so desolate as the squawking of seagulls?

The sound of a human voice took me completely by surprise.

'Hello, Emma.'

It was Richard.

'I didn't know you were coming,' I gasped.

'What, not come for the gallery opening? I wouldn't miss it for worlds.'

Even he only cared about the gallery. He hadn't come to see me. So instead of jumping up and asking him excited questions as I usually did, I just went on sitting on my rock. Richard sat down beside me.

'I'm sorry you've been ill. You should have told me.'

'I'm all right now,' I replied with a martyred air.

'Post-flu depression?' he inquired sympathetically. 'Island blues?'

'Just because I don't leap about like a young goat all the time,' I began furiously.

'Emma,' said Richard, 'don't be like that. What's the matter?'

'Nothing's the matter. Or everything. I don't know.'

'Tell me.'

'There's nothing to tell. I'm just – sick of everything.' In spite of myself my voice trembled. I blinked my eyes very fast and continued looking out to sea.

'Are you fed up with school?'

'I'm not going back.'

'You did quite well with your O-levels,' Richard said, 'but what on earth made you fail Latin?'

'I hate Latin.'

'But you might need it for University.'

'I'm not going to University,' I snapped.

'Why?'

'I don't want to. I've left school.'

'What? You're mad!' exploded Richard.

'Just because I'm not like you. I don't want to live in a horrible hostel in Oban.'

'You're being puerile.'

'All right. I'm puerile. Thank you very much.'

'But Emma—'

'You're always telling me to live my own life. Well, I'm going to.'

Richard kept his temper with difficulty. He whistled a few bars of something or other and then spoke in a different tone of voice.

'Why didn't you reply to my letter? Or did having flu put it out of your mind?'

'But I did reply,' I said, and then I remembered. I had written the letter but had not posted it. I had been going to buy envelopes on the day my flu started. The letter must still

59

be in my drawer. I felt a flicker of hope and then quickly banished it.

'You don't want me,' I muttered.

'Oh, for goodness' sake,' Richard said impatiently. 'Don't be such a clown. Would I have asked you if I didn't mean it?'

'You'll have Pauline.'

'So what?'

'So what!'

'Emma, I could shake you,' Richard said angrily, and he went as far as taking me by the shoulders but when he saw my face he didn't shake me.

'You're a silly goose,' he said gently. 'Now don't think I'm going to swear undying devotion or tell you that my holiday will be ruined without the company of my beloved sister but – I'd like you to come. Honestly.'

'Patsy and Stephen won't be able to spare me. They need me to work in the gallery.'

'If you've been looking and behaving like this for any length of time they'll be glad to see the back of you,' Richard retorted. 'Come, stiffen the upper lip, put your shoulder to the wheel and your hand to the plough and for goodness' sake smile.'

I looked at Richard and tried to smile but it was a half-hearted affair.

Richard pulled me to my feet. 'Come on, my bottom is beginning to grow barnacles.'

We walked slowly back to the gallery and I introduced Richard to Vanessa.

'Hmm,' said Richard, who wasn't interested in babies. 'Looks more or less the usual shape and colour.'

'But she's beautiful,' I protested, picking her up.

'Yes, yes, of course.'

He admired the gallery far more, squinted at the pictures in a professional way and made sensible remarks about the pottery. I felt left-out and lonely all over again so I sat on the step, cuddling Vanessa, and ignoring the conversation.

Suddenly Richard sat down at the piano and began to play a pseudo-jazz tune, singing in a pseudo-jazz voice:

'She's got those far off island blues,
'She's got those doggone island blues,
She's wasting away
From day to day
Cos she's got those island blues.
My baby can't eat or drink,
My baby can't laugh or think,
She gets a pain
In the wind and the rain
Cos she's got those island blues.'

'Shut up!' I shouted furiously.

'What is all this?' asked Aunt Patsy.

'Island blues, huh?' said Stephen.

Richard crashed into discords and then stopped. Everyone looked at me.

'My baby, beg pardon, my little sister,' Richard said, 'has got post-flu depression, island blues, what you will. She needs a holiday.'

'A holiday. Of course. Why didn't we think of it before?' exclaimed Aunt Patsy.

'You've been overworking her, I told you to stop,' said Stephen.

'She's dripping with self-pity, martyrdom and inferiority,' continued Richard.

'Shut up!' I yelled.

'I propose,' said Richard in his most lordly voice, 'to whisk her away in a four-wheeled chariot, a vintage Austin to be exact, and to distract her with the wonder and mystery of continental travel. We may take in, as the Americans say, Salzburg, and then on to Brno, Czechoslovakia, the birthplace of a composer called Janáček where there is a festival in his honour.'

'That sounds a splendid idea,' said Aunt Patsy.

'If she refuses to allow Oban High School to cultivate her tiny mind,' continued Richard spitefully, 'I see that I shall have to take charge. If anyone knows of let or hindrance to this plan let him or her speak now or for ever hold his peace.'

'I don't see why not,' said Stephen.

'I won't be organized in front of my face,' I protested feebly.

'You'll do what you're told,' said Richard. 'We are your elders and betters. We know what is good for you.'

'I'm going to give Vanessa her bath,' I said and left them to it.

Secretly I felt very cheered up. People did care about me after all.

I bathed Vanessa with special efficiency. I cuddled her and sang to her; washed and powdered her; dressed her in her night-clothes, murmuring:

'Darling Vanessa, you're sweet, I adore you. I won't be away for long, I promise.'

Vanessa reached up and caught a bit of my hair and tugged it. How strong she was! I breathed in the delicious smell of clean baby and popped her in her cot. She put her thumb in her mouth and looked at me slyly with her periwinkle blue eyes.

'Perhaps, Vanessa,' I told her, 'life is not quite so bleak as it was half an hour ago.'

When I went downstairs they were all in the kitchen drinking whisky. Everything had been settled and I did not feel strong enough to complain.

Very gradually I began to look forward to the trip. Stephen, who had been to Salzburg, told me about the little town set in a hollow of the mountains; about the Glockenspiel Café where you drank chocolate with whipped cream, served with a little glass of iced water; about delicious cakes, wild strawberries and Wiener Schnitzels; about the lakes nearby where you could swim, about handsome boys in leather shorts.

'It's a pity the Festival isn't until August,' said Richard, 'but we'll get all the music we want in Brno.'

I was so bemused by these descriptions that I absent-mindedly ate a huge supper and bullied everyone into washing it up. And when I climbed upstairs to bed there was hardly a trace of my post-flu depression or island blues.

Or I thought they had disappeared. I was staring into my mirror and telling my reflection, 'You're going to Salzburg.

You're going to Czechoslovakia,' when they all started up again.

Since we had been on Stranday I had not bothered about my appearance. I just wore clothes that were suitable for the climate and for my chores when I was not in school uniform. And now I realized how very unsuitable they would be for holiday gadding.

I was thin and pale, my hair was long and unkempt, I hadn't a dress to my name, or sandals or a coat or a handbag. Or anything. Pauline would be sleek and fashionable even in disarray – I just knew – with her eyes made up and all the latest gimmicky clothes which we read about in the magazines but never had a chance of seeing or buying on Stranday. As for Bill, if he was Richard's friend he would probably be a terrific intellectual and my only hope of keeping my end up would have been to look ravishingly beautiful. As it was, I would just be Richard's little sister that everyone must be kind to. 'She's very sweet really,' they would say. I was almost sixteen and I looked about ten, an unattractive ten at that.

I stuck out my tongue at myself and then crept miserably into bed.

Chapter Ten

I WOKE up the next morning very sober and sensible and full of good resolutions. If I could not be beautiful abroad I could at any rate be useful at home. So I collected the milk and prepared breakfast, something I had not done since before I was ill. It gave me a very saintly feeling.

All the same I would have liked to discuss my clothes problems with someone. Richard simply did not notice what people wore and hardly what they looked like. I had asked him about Pauline:

'What's she like?'

'Hair like golden syrup, eyes like treacle toffee.'

'What sort of things does she wear?'

'Oh clothes, I suppose. I've never noticed.'

Aunt Patsy would be just as bad, I knew, and Stephen who just conceivably might know better, could hardly be expected to waste his hard-earned cash on me. As usual I never knew quite how rich or poor we were. Some of the things we did struck me as downright extravagant – like the drastic alterations to the gallery – yet on the other hand none of us had had any new clothes for ages; we lived mostly on soup, cheese and eggs; we had no telephone and the kitchen stove was antediluvian. To ask for, say, thirty pounds for clothes might break the bank. And I had only a few shillings saved because I had never succeeded in training Aunt Patsy to give me regular pocket-money.

But today the sun shone, the sea glittered, sea-gulls swooped, clouds sailed, leaves danced in the wind. It was impossible not to hope for the best. After I'd eaten my breakfast I seized Vanessa from Aunt Patsy and kissed her behind her funny little ears.

'I want a housework squad,' I said bossily, prancing round the room with Vanessa. 'Everything, but everything, is going to be scrubbed, polished, tidied, dusted, swept, to be ready for the opening next week.'

'Oh no,' groaned Aunt Patsy.

'Oh yes,' I retorted, 'I shall go and drag my lazy brother from the piano.'

'Emma is fully recovered,' said Stephen. 'I might have guessed what the result would be. But I too shall play my part. And one of the things you both need is a hair-cut. Failing superior skill I shall do it myself. Which of you will be first?'

'Not me,' I said, edging out of the room.

'Then I shall start with you, Patsy,' Stephen said. 'Where are the scissors?'

I left them to it and put Vanessa in her pram, rocking it gently until she fell asleep. Then, looking up, I noticed a strange collection of people getting out of the minibus at the top of our track. I rushed back to the cottage.

'Are you expecting anyone?' I accused Aunt Patsy.

'Not a soul.'

'Not guilty,' said Stephen, snipping away.

'Well, they're coming, just the same.'

They followed me out of the house and we watched a dozen people walking down our track.

'There's the *Scotsman* critic,' said Stephen.

'And Jim and Dave.'

'And that man from the Cosmos Gallery in Glasgow.'

'And that woman – whatsername? – who bought one of your pictures last year.'

'And—' we looked at each other in bewilderment as Richard came out of the gallery, announcing:

'Ah, the first customers are arriving.'

'But it's not today,' said Aunt Patsy. 'It's next Thursday.'

'They must have made a mistake,' said Stephen.

'Of course it's today,' said Richard crossly. 'Why do you think I'm here.'

'It's next week,' repeated Aunt Patsy.

'June the twenty-first,' added Stephen.

'But today *is* June the twenty-first,' Richard shouted.

'It can't be,' said Aunt Patsy.

'But it is!'

Aunt Patsy and Stephen closed their eyes as if to say: 'How stupid can some people get?' when the visitors were upon us. There were handshakes, friendly questions, congratulations, comments on the weather. Everyone appeared to be under the impression that it was June the twenty-first, the day of the opening.

'Listen,' said Aunt Patsy faintly, 'could one of you tell me quietly, please, what today's date is?'

'June the twenty-first,' chorused everyone.

'Oh!'

Stephen and Aunt Patsy and I looked at each other despairingly; we began to giggle and then to laugh.

'I told you,' I said between snorts and splutters, 'what would happen if we came to live on an island. We're not an hour out or a day out, we're a week out.'

We were falling about with laughter until the visitors began to see the joke and they laughed too. By the time order had been restored Donald the Minibus had arrived with a second load of visitors. We became hysterical all over again.

But everyone rose to the occasion. Stephen formally opened the gallery and then dashed off with Donald to get in supplies of food and drink, leaving Richard in charge. Aunt Patsy started a huge pan of soup. I whisked round the house, not cleaning in any thorough way but simply putting offending objects out of sight. When I reappeared the *Scotsman* critic was joggling Vanessa's pram because she had begun to cry. Inside the gallery Jim was sitting at the loom finishing my rug and the woman who had bought one of Stephen's pictures the previous year was taking out her cheque book to pay for another.

In the evening some of our island friends arrived, including a stray archaeologist or two, and a party developed. After I had made sandwiches, poured beer and washed up glasses non-stop for hours I began to feel terribly tired so I decided to sit on my rock awhile to recover. I walked very slowly down the path to the sea, breathing deeply while the party noises receded and the sea noises took over.

Then I noticed that someone else had escaped from the party too and was standing looking out to sea, his shirt very white in the dusk. Hearing my footsteps crunching on the shingle he turned round and I recognized one of the stray archaeologists.

'You're Emma, aren't you?' he said.

'Mm,' I agreed. I really wanted to be by myself and not to have to make conversation with a strange young man.

'My name's Alastair and I'm with this archaeological outfit.'

'I know.'

'Mr Kilpatrick thought you might like a job – we're going to be working here all summer. It will be rather fun.'

Somebody else was trying to organize my life for me.

'I'm going abroad with my brother,' I said briefly.

'Lucky you. But what about when you come back? I'm

66

just part of the advance guard but the rest of the students and volunteers will be arriving soon and we could do with extra help.'

I peered at his face to see if there were any indications that this was a put-up job but it was too dark to see more than a white blur. Certainly his voice sounded sincere.

'What have you discovered so far?'

'A burial ground up near the loch. At least we think we have.'

'What would I have to do? Dig with a teaspoon?'

Alastair laughed. 'Roughly,' he said.

'I might like to,' I said slowly.

'Good-O, I'll put your name down, shall I?'

'All right.' It seemed less trouble to agree. I could always change my mind later on.

'This is a marvellous place,' Alastair said. 'Fancy being able to live here all the year round!'

'Where do you live?'

'Glasgow, and I've got two more years of University there.'

'I've just done O-levels and I'm sick of school,' I burst out.

'It does get rather dreary,' agreed Alastair sympathetically. 'Sometimes I feel I'll be an old man before I finish with exams. But digs are great. Last year . . .'

It was suddenly very peaceful sitting on my rock, listening to the swish of the sea and Alastair's voice telling me about digs he had been on in the past. In the dark I did not need to feel self-conscious about my appearance, and talking to a complete stranger who did not know any of my problems made it possible for me to ignore them, too. I imagined myself discovering some brooch or breastplate or spear. It would be gloriously exciting. I did not want to sit still any longer.

'Are you hungry?' I asked. 'I'm ravenous.'

'Now I come to think of it, I am rather.'

So we went back into the cottage and I made fried eggs and coffee. Now I could see Alastair clearly I liked what I saw. He was thin, not particularly tall, with very bright grey

67

eyes, dark hair and long curly eyelashes. I wished that I was not so scruffily dressed but he did not appear to notice so I stopped worrying and began to tell him about life on the island, our misadventurous journey, about the piano being lost and all the other funny things that had happened to us.

'Go on, this is marvellous,' he said, every time I stopped.

We were still talking when Aunt Patsy came in to give Vanessa her last feed.

'Has she been quiet, Emma?' she asked anxiously.

'Er, yes,' I replied guiltily because I had completely forgotten about Vanessa.

She hurried upstairs and I heard her utter a small shriek.

'What's the matter?' I cried. Had Vanessa fallen out of her cot, swallowed a safety pin, choked on a ribbon?

Then I heard Aunt Patsy laughing as she came downstairs holding Vanessa, so I knew nothing dreadful could have happened.

'I'd completely forgotten,' she said, 'Stephen never finished cutting my hair and here I've been all day in this lop-sided state. Why didn't anyone tell me?'

We cackled with laughter.

'Probably everyone thought it was a quaint native custom,' said Alastair. 'I know I did.'

'Cheeky.'

While we were explaining to her about the dig, Richard arrived.

'They've settled down for an all-night session,' he said, 'but I'm exhausted. Is there any grub going?'

Then Stephen came in, breathless and excited.

'I've sold five pictures,' he said triumphantly. 'Five pictures! Isn't it great? Emma, I've been thinking about you.'

'Me? Why?'

'For the past year you have been head cook and bottle-washer, nursemaid, odd job man and what have you – all, I may say, unpaid. Will you allow me to present you with a small sum representing your back wages?'

'About time too,' said Aunt Patsy unjustly.

I blushed with pleasure and embarrassment and made unconvincing protests.

'It struck me,' continued Stephen, 'that if you are holidaying abroad you will need some additions to your wardrobe.'

'Mmmm,' I invited.

'You must go back to Edinburgh with Richard and buy yourself some gaudy skirts and topless tops and psychedelic sandals and whatever else is current fashion.'

I purred.

'Oh Lord,' growled Richard. 'I'm not going shopping for all the music in Czechoslovakia.'

'You're a blind boorish fellow. But I know no female will go anywhere without a complete change of wardrobe. Not for nothing have I laboured on popular magazines. Isn't that true, Emma?'

'Yes,' I grinned.

'I give up,' said Richard. 'Now am I going to get any grub or not?'

'Get it yourself,' I said smartly. 'I'm busy.'

Stephen was making a list: two dresses, skirt and different tops, a showerproof coat, cardigan, stockings, sandals, shoes, handbag, underclothing, swimsuit, he wrote.

'Don't forget make-up,' said Aunt Patsy who was feeding Vanessa and being, to my surprise, extremely helpful. 'And stick to one range of colours, Emma, different shades of orange for instance.'

'To go with her gorgeous hair,' said Alastair.

'Gorgeous,' I spluttered unbelievingly, 'it's like a haystack, it's like spaniels' ears.'

'Stephen will oblige,' Aunt Patsy said, 'but persuade him to cut both sides this time.'

Slowly I began to see myself with short tidy hair again, wearing an orange dress.

'Perhaps something in shocking pink just to make the boys sit up,' mused Aunt Patsy.

'I am not going to wear shocking pink,' I said firmly, looking at the list which seemed to be getting longer and longer. 'Oh dear, it's going to cost a terrible lot.'

'Old Minnie the Moaner,' jeered Stephen. 'We'll put you to work again when you get back.'

'But—' I began. Perhaps I ought not to go on the dig after all.

'She's going on a dig,' cut in Aunt Patsy swiftly.

Alastair explained and Stephen shrugged his shoulders.

'OK. We'll live on nettle soup and salt herring until I sell some more pictures.'

But he smiled his particularly nice smile so that I knew he did not mind and I relaxed.

There are some moments when happiness is almost something you can touch, like holding a big golden orange. I looked at them all – Aunt Patsy with her funny lop-sided hair and Vanessa leaning milkily against her; Stephen, writing my list in his black elegant writing, his face still flushed with excitement because of selling his pictures; Richard shovelling in bacon and egg but looking up to give me a glint of approval when he heard about the dig; Alastair who was not yet a friend but who might easily become one. I thought of Salzburg, sitting in a café in my new clothes, drinking chocolate with whipped cream, of swimming and going to concerts; of taking part in the dig and coming up with some fabulous treasure.

I loved my cottage and my island but they would still be there when I got back.

In the silence we could hear the wild noise of the party in the gallery. Someone had started playing the accordion and Donald the Minibus was wailing on his pipes.

Alastair looked at me inquiringly.

'Let's go and dance,' he said.

'What me, looking like this?'

'Yes, you, looking like that.'

'I'll come too,' said Richard, 'the piano needs exercise.'

We jostled out into the garden, laughing and tripping over things in the dark.

Chapter Eleven

Two days later Richard returned to Edinburgh but not before we had had a tremendous row about my education.

'Can't you and Stephen knock some sense into this silly child's head?' Richard asked belligerently. 'It's ludicrous to think of leaving school at fifteen.'

'Stop trying to run my life,' I snapped back. 'And anyhow I'll be sixteen in August.'

'I honestly think you'll regret it, Emma,' said Stephen.

'I left school at fifteen and I've never regretted it,' said Aunt Patsy.

'But you went to Art College at a later date,' said Richard.

'Why shouldn't Emma do the same?'

'With all respect to you, my dear Aunt,' said Richard, 'Emma is not artistic and never will be.'

'Charming!' I muttered. 'A fat lot you know about it.'

'Emma ought to go to University,' said Richard.

'Well, she can always go if she changes her mind,' said Aunt Patsy magnanimously, as if I'd be doing some University a favour.

'It will be hard enough to get a place if she starts applying herself now,' said Richard, 'but if she takes a couple of years off kicking her heels in idleness—' he shrugged his shoulders, 'you've no idea of the competition.'

'Richard's right,' murmured Stephen, 'but the thing is, does Emma want to go to University?'

'She's not old enough to know what she wants,' Richard shouted. 'You're in charge. You must exert your authority.'

'I don't want to go,' I shouted back. 'And I'm never idle. I work jolly hard. Stephen needs me in the gallery, don't you, Stephen?'

'Look,' said Aunt Patsy, 'I have no intention of exerting

authority. There's enough bullying in the world without my adding to it.'

'I give up,' Richard groaned. He got up from the table and went over to the window – even his shoulders looked angry – 'you're all mad.'

Stephen tried again.

'Let's be reasonable,' he said. 'Emma's been ill and she's in no fit state to make up her mind about anything. What's more, she's had to face a lot of changes in her life in the last two years. Maybe she needs a little peace and quiet to recover.'

'Exactly,' said Aunt Patsy triumphantly.

'Quiet, Patsy,' Stephen barked. 'I don't in the least mind exerting authority when it's needed. But in this case I suggest leaving the subject alone for the duration of the summer holidays to give Emma time to think seriously about her future without pressure from any of us.'

Richard turned round.

'Can I ask a question?' he said quietly.

'Of course.'

'Do you honestly think that helping to run the gallery can ever be Emma's real work? Will it ever be in a position to pay her a living wage?'

'A living wage,' snorted Aunt Patsy with contempt while Stephen shushed her again.

Although I did not like being quarrelled over, it was nice to feel important and I listened eagerly for Stephen's reply.

'No,' he said slowly. 'No to both questions. But it can give her a breathing space – if that is what she needs. We may have to make other plans ourselves when the five years are up, though the last time I heard from Dennis he sounded pretty rapturous about waffles and clam chowder and bourbon on the rocks.'

'All right,' said Richard at length. 'I agree to leave the subject alone for the present.' He smiled rather stiffly and came back to the table to give my hair a friendly tug. 'Cheer up, little sister, no one's going to chain you to your desk.'

I tried to find out what I really did want. It was true that I was not artistic and it was also true that I was in a confused state of mind. If only the island school could have prepared me for University entrance it would have been different, but the thought of yet another change in my life terrified me. Some people are adventurous and some are not. As Mother had always said, I was a creature of habit. I wanted to live a settled life. And nowadays whenever I got settled somewhere I was hustled off to settle somewhere else.

I also had a definite feeling of obligation – that I ought to pay back Aunt Patsy for having given me a home when I was an orphan. She would deny it, of course, but that made it all the more important. Vanessa and the gallery were my duty as well as my inclination.

Before I came to Stranday I had been completely convinced about the importance of education and passing exams but suddenly I had seen how unimportant it was compared to being happy. Now I did not want to miss a moment of island life with Aunt Patsy, Stephen and Vanessa. I agreed to shelve any decision until after the holiday but I knew I would never change my mind.

So I went back to Edinburgh with Richard and it felt most peculiar not to stay at the High House. Richard's digs were in Marchmont, a gloomy place to live. It was a dark grimy house with bulging bay windows and his landlady was the sort of person who shuffles about in carpet slippers all day, wearing a flowered overall and curlers in her hair. Richard had one big room almost filled up by his grand piano and a sagging sofa, a small bedroom, and a rather nasty smelly kitchen and bathroom which he had to share with three other students. I was tempted to start painting and to insist on new curtains but there were only two days before we travelled to London to meet Pauline and Bill. And first I had to have my hair cut and to buy my new clothes.

The hairdressers I chose was bright and crowded, reeking with scent and hot towels and other hairdressing smells. The attendants seemed to be young and supercilious, with elaborate hair styles. They were all chattering to each other and to the customers so I felt very plain and young and inadequate.

'How do you want it, dear?' said mine, whose name was Belinda, combing my shaggy locks in an absent-minded way and carrying on a conversation over one shoulder with another assistant whose name was Valerie.

I gulped, staring at myself in the glass, all scarlet and shining from the sizzling shampoo.

'Valerie, your lady's here,' sang out the voice of the girl at the reception desk over the intercom and Valerie disappeared. Thank goodness. Perhaps Belinda would concentrate on me now.

'Short,' I said desperately.

Belinda took out scissors and a comb with a bored expression so I tried again to make her take a personal interest.

'I want to look nice,' I pleaded. 'I've been staying in the country where I couldn't get it done and now I'm going on a holiday abroad.'

'That'll be nice,' said Belinda without changing her expression. But she started cutting, talking this time over her other shoulder to an assistant who was plastering dye with a big paintbrush on to an old lady's head.

'My daughter's getting married and I want to look my best,' babbled the old lady. 'I've got the sweetest hat.'

I gritted my teeth and watched Belinda in the mirror, slashing away at my hair. Then she stuck in enormous rollers, so tight that the skin of my face was stretched almost to breaking point.

'All right, dear,' she said absently. 'This way please!' And she led me to a dryer, clamped it over my head, threw a couple of magazines at me and disappeared.

My spirits sank lower and lower. Probably I would look so dreadful that even Richard would notice and refuse to take me with him. Bill would sneer and as for Pauline, with her hair like golden syrup, she would laugh her head off. It was just my luck to have curly hair when straight hair was all the fashion.

When Belinda unclamped the dryer and took me back to the other seat I was beyond speech and beyond looking in the mirror. I just sat, examining my hands, while Belinda brushed and combed and fiddled until she said languidly:

'There. How do you like that?'

I looked up and to my enormous astonishment the result was like those before-and-after advertisements. I had been transformed.

My hair had been shaped to my head, not in curls so much as rough feathers, brushed forward from the crown into a sort of uneven fringe. No longer did I look ten years old. At a pinch I might look seventeen.

Radiantly I thanked Belinda, paid the enormous bill and rushed off to find some clothes worthy of my hair. I bought a chocolate-coloured plain linen dress, a very gay one in patterns of yellow and orange, and a light brown canvas showerproof coat. Then I dashed back to Marchmont to Richard.

He was fortunately out so I had time to change into my brown dress and to experiment with my new make-up – the eye-liner took ages because my hand kept shaking with excitement – before he came home.

'Well?' I asked triumphantly, parading round the room.

'I say,' said Richard, blinking, 'you do look different.'

'Different better or different worse?'

'Different better, of course, you goose. I suppose now I shall have to take you out to supper. You can hardly bend over a hot stove in that get-up.'

So we went out to a small Indian restaurant and ate such hot curry that I had to drink several glasses of water afterwards to cool my mouth down. There were one or two people there who knew Richard and they looked me up and down in such a way that I realized my new appearance was going to be a success.

The next day, after finishing my shopping, I helped Richard to pack which entailed a lot of argument as Richard's idea of packing is to put a clean shirt and a toothbrush into a rucksack and then fill up with musical scores.

'I've got to take some Janáček scores with me,' he protested.

'You've got to take some clean underwear too,' I told him firmly.

'Oh don't fuss.'

'I'm not fussing. I'm just being sensible.'

In the end we effected a compromise.

We caught the night train down and then a bus to Pauline's house in Canonbury where we were going to have breakfast and to meet Bill.

It was the first time I had been in London since my parents died and the moment I stepped on to the gritty platform at King's Cross and smelt the station smells and saw the jostling early morning crowds and the familiar red buses, I was quite overwhelmed. London had been my home for such a long time that the Edinburgh Emma and the island Emma faded away and once again I was ten years old, hurrying home from school to find Mother with my tea ready on the table; once again I was helping Daddy weed the flower-beds; once again I was choosing a family treat like to the zoo or visiting Kew Gardens. I longed desperately to turn the clock back to when life was simple and I had no decisions to make.

'Don't,' said Richard who always knows what I am feeling.

'I can't help it. It's being in London.'

'I don't mean it's bad to remember. But look forward as well.'

'I'll try.'

Then he began to talk about Janaček and how he was the most important composer of this century; how if it was humanly possible we'd go to a superb opera called 'Katia Kabanova'; and though I was not specially interested I had time to pull myself together before I met Pauline.

We got off the bus and walked up a nearby street until we reached a tall thin house. We rang the bell and waited. Naturally I was feeling extremely nervous because if Pauline did not like me – or if I did not like her – the whole holiday would be spoiled. But the moment she opened the door and flung her arms round Richard, saying: 'Richard, angel-face, oh isn't this exciting?' I realized that it would be easy to like her.

Then she grabbed me and pulled me inside.

'Emma,' she exclaimed, 'of course. Now stand beside your brother. Yes, you're much prettier than he is.'

'My aim,' said Richard with dignity, 'is not to look pretty but to look distinguished.'

'Same coloured hair but no freckles,' Pauline went on.

'Freckles are a sign of intelligence,' put in Richard quickly.

'Anyhow, come on down and have breakfast. You must both be starving. I know I always am after a night on the train.'

So we went downstairs to a big basement kitchen and sat down while Pauline made toast and coffee and boiled eggs. She chattered on but I left Richard to do the talking while I studied her.

She was slender and her hair was long and smooth and blonde, really more honey-coloured than golden-syrup-coloured. She had a triangular-shaped face and her two front teeth, instead of being straight across, were set at an angle so that when she spoke it looked as though she were taking neat little bites. She was wearing a dark-blue cotton dressing-gown and shabby mules.

'Oh I'm glad your aunt let you come,' she said to me, 'because I couldn't have gone away with two men without another girl, and of my fellow students one has spots, one smells as if she's been eating onions, and there's another who talks about her dog all the time. Oh, they're a dreary crowd.'

'You must be exaggerating,' protested Richard.

'Well, maybe a teeny bit. Ah, here come the parents.'

Richard and I got up to shake hands and then the conversation died down. We talked politely about the trip and our route and the weather and they gave us all the usual advice which is so useless because by the time you need it it's usually too late. So I was quite relieved when a car hooted outside and Richard exclaimed: 'That's Bill.'

Bill had been to the same boarding school as Richard and now he was studying computers at London University. He had a manner, a sort of acquired polish, as if he had been taught all the correct things to say and do without taking account of his own personality. How different from poor stammering Douglas he was, I thought, Douglas who had no polish at all. And yet I was more conscious of the genuine Douglas than I ever became of the genuine Bill. He was very charming and gay and polite; he used an elaborate slang that was half school, I think, and half his own. He was well-read and hardworking yet he pretended that he never read anything except James Bond, that he spent all his time drinking in pubs or watching football and that his only ambition was to marry a rich heiress so that he could sail round the world on a luxury yacht.

But I did not know all that then. My first impression was just of someone with a white-toothed smile, a careless handshake, very long legs and the fact that he called Pauline's father 'Sir'.

'If you'll excuse us, sir,' he said, 'we'll have to be tumbling aboard and I'd like to get the gear stowed. Now girls, keep your luggage to a minimum, no hat-boxes, tape-recorders, tennis racquets or other fripperies.'

'Come and help me, Emma,' said Pauline, leading the way upstairs. 'And you'd probably like a wash. What are you going to wear for the journey? I thought jeans and shirts would be best, then we can keep our smart things for going to cafés and concerts.'

In about an hour we had arranged ourselves in the car, Bill at the wheel, Richard sitting beside him with the map, and us girls in the back. We left in a flurry of injunctions from Pauline's parents not to lose our Travellers' Cheques and visas, not to drink unboiled water, not to drive too fast on the motorway, not to ... not to ... not ...

'Coo,' said Bill. 'Parents.'

'They're very sweet really,' defended Pauline. 'They just can't help worrying.'

'Parents,' said Bill, 'should be kept in order.'

Chapter Twelve

WE travelled to Salzburg via Ostend, Frankfurt and Munich and it was all very exciting but I do not really care for long car journeys. You get cramp or indigestion from sitting crumpled up; you're either too hot or too cold; and at night, although you're terribly tired, you can't sleep because you go on driving. As for being abroad for the first time, which should have been exciting in itself, after I had looked at farms and cottages and villages and towns and churches and castles and woods and hills and the long blank stretches of motorway for hours on end, the scenery went into a blur and it was more interesting to talk and sing.

Bill was the sort of boy who had, so to speak, stepped into a car straight from his pram and since he lived in a big house in the country he had been able to learn to drive on a private road and had passed his test without turning a hair on his seventeenth birthday. Nothing worried him and he fortunately did not spend the time cursing other drivers as so many people do.

He and Richard invented two awful P. G. Wodehouse-characters who talked nonsense to each other by the hour.

'I say, old boy, time for a spot of tiffin, what?'

'Bung ho.'

'The natives in these parts look friendly, I fancy.'

'If not we'll unfurl the jolly old Union Jack.'

'They can't mistake an officer and a gentleman.'

'It's breeding that counts. I remember my uncle telling me that when he was in Poonah . . .'

Now that I have written this down I realize it is not funny at all, but at the time it made us laugh. Pauline had her own brand of nonsense, too, but I will not try to describe it as it would give the impression that she was a silly girl when in fact she was extremely clever. She and Richard read scores together sometimes, singing or doodling the various parts.

And she called Richard by all sorts of ridiculous nicknames and endearments which I would blush to repeat.

'Do you honestly like being called "angel"?' I asked him.

'Pauline is one of the few girls who has recognized my divine qualities,' Richard said.

'One of the few? Who are the others?' demanded Pauline.

'Oh, Juliet and Pamela and Cynthia and Myrtle and . . .' listed Richard until she cuffed him.

Even I thought up one or two things to say to make them laugh so I began to feel witty as well as attractive.

Another way we passed the time was by singing rounds as Pauline and Richard knew a great many and Bill and I were quick to learn. There was one very sad one about a man who had to sell his horse, and the melting way we sang:

> *'Friend, old friend, the children want their meat.*
> *In another stable you'll have corn to eat . . .'*

almost brought tears to my eyes.

But my favourite was a German one about nightingales, by Mozart, and when it got going there would be one of us doing slow bass notes while the rest chirruped up in the treble.

We decided to stop just outside Salzburg on the shores of a little lake and to put up our own tents instead of using the proper camping-sites as we had done on the journey to save time. There was a small saw-mill nearby and Bill, who spoke good German, asked permission from a melancholy old man with drooping whiskers and a grey jacket with horn buttons. In spite of looking so gloomy, he agreed, and even sold us some eggs and some corn on the cob, after which we all shook hands and said 'Grüss Gott' which is what you always say in Austria.

So we pitched our tents to face the lake, built a fireplace with stones, collected water in our plastic can and decided to have a swim before supper. Floating on my back in the delicious silky water, with the sun hot on my face, I felt calm and serene and brimful of holiday happiness. I thought affectionately of Aunt Patsy and Stephen and Vanessa but just for once it was wonderful to have no chores or responsibilities.

After our swim the boys went off to buy wine while Pauline and I got the fire going and began to cook supper. The corn had to be boiled in relays because the saucepan would only hold two at a time. With it we ate huge slabs of rye bread and butter and salami.

'This is a seductive little wine,' said Bill appreciatively, 'let me fill your glass, Emma.'

'I hope you're not trying to make my little sister drunk,' Richard reproved him.

'Not drunk, just uplifted.'

'Besides,' I added, 'we've been instructed not to drink the water.'

So we sat round the fire drinking, watching the pink sunset clouds reflected in the lake and singing our nightingale song very softly and sweetly.

The next day we drove into Salzburg and it was just as I had imagined it: the mountains all round, steep streets, and cafés where you could sit outside under striped awnings or umbrellas. We sat in the Glockenspiel Café, drinking chocolate with whipped cream, laughing at the other tourists. For there were tourists everywhere, in funny hats, carrying Air Company hold-alls stuffed with paper handkerchiefs, buying or writing postcards, taking photographs of each other and studying their guide books.

'But we are tourists too,' I ventured. I was writing postcards myself, to Aunt Patsy and Stephen and Vanessa.

'Tourists are like foreigners,' said Bill, 'other people, never oneself.'

'Still I'd sooner go back to our lake and swim than follow this merry throng around, studying points of interest,' said Pauline.

'I'd like to hear some music,' retorted Richard.

So we found a ticket office but the only tickets that were not impossibly expensive were two for standing room in a church called The Dom where the Brahms Requiem was being performed.

81

'You and Pauline go,' said Bill, 'and I shall take Emma out to supper. I fancy that the cuisine is fairly reputable at a joint called Peter's Keller.'

At first I felt rather self-conscious about being alone with Bill. He was so much older (eighteen) and I thought he might feel it was undignified to take someone's little sister out. What on earth would we talk about? I was not very good at talking nonsense on my own and the established gambit of asking him about his work would hardly be successful in this case since my entire knowledge of computers would fit on to the head of a pin, and you have to know something about a subject before asking questions.

The restaurant was in a sort of cellar and the dark walls contrasted well with the glittering white tablecloths and sparkling cutlery.

'I say, do you know anything about this Janaček chap?' he asked me, after we had sat down and I was still wondering how to start the conversation.

'Not much. Do you?'

'Not really in my line. I thought he was strictly for egg-heads.'

'So you haven't heard this opera, Katia something or other, that Richard is keen on?'

'Now I come to think of it,' said Bill carelessly, 'someone did drag me to the Czech Nat Op, last time it was in England. Some quite tasty singing as far as I can remember.'

'Can you speak any Czech?'

'A few words, a few words – please, thank you and beer. That should see me through. Now what are you going to eat?'

'Schnitzel,' I said, 'and that's my only German word except for Grüss Gott.'

'We are obviously ideally suited,' Bill said, 'we could travel round the world on our joint knowledge. And that, my dear Emma, is what makes us different from the ordinary tourists. We take trouble to acquire the native lingo.'

The schnitzels arrived on huge plates, very thin tender slices of veal fried in breadcrumbs, with blobs of different vegetables and fruit arranged round them. They were delicious. Then we had pineapple water ices. Meanwhile Bill was asking me about life on the island and I was able to follow his example and not make the mistake of telling him what it was really like. For instance I referred to Vanessa merely as 'my aunt's small brat', and Stephen's pictures as 'weird and avant garde'.

'A gallery on an island?' Bill exclaimed incredulously, 'does it bring in any lolly?'

'Not much to date.'

'You will have to beguile some millionaire to anchor his yacht there and while he is feeding deep upon your peerless eyes, Stephen can flog him the odd masterpiece.'

'Do you know any likely millionaires?'

'One or two, but all they want to buy are oil wells and insurance companies. Still, apart from beguiling millionaires what are your plans, Emma?'

I looked at him sharply to see if perhaps Richard had told him about my wanting to leave school and asked him to intervene. But his eyes were as blue and lazy as ever.

'What else is there?' I yawned. I was keeping my end of the conversation up extremely well, I thought.

'True, true. Just what I tell my young sister. But she's the intellectual type. Wants a career.'

For a moment I was going to say indignantly, 'Well, what's wrong with that?' and then I realized I would be playing straight into his hands – if Richard had confided in him – so I said instead:

'How energetic!'

'Well, she says, as I believe Jane Austen also remarked, that there are simply not enough rich handsome young men to go round all the pretty girls who deserve them.'

Again I observed him narrowly. I had never before had a conversation with someone who deliberately said what he did not mean. It was like a game and I was not sure if I was winning. I needed to say something that would indicate my superior intellectual ideas at the same time as affecting to despise them. But I could not think of the right remark.

By this time we had finished dinner and Bill paid. I wanted to apologize for all the money I was costing him but it might have sounded naïve. We wandered round the town for a bit until we discovered a small hall where they were putting on a puppet play and decided to visit it. The play was all about Mozart in Salzburg, in very idiomatic Austrian-German, which Bill translated for my benefit. There were a lot of jokes about rain and I gathered that there was something special about Salzburg rain and laughed too. When we came out I realized why, because it was pelting with the thickest, wettest rain imaginable. We dashed for the car, parking it near The Dom, to wait for Richard and Pauline.

As soon as they appeared, we roared away down the narrow street. 'Home,' said Bill. 'Have you chaps had any grub?'

It turned out that they had had frankfurters and potato salad and though they pretended to be very jealous of our schnitzels I could see they did not really care. They had had Brahms' Requiem and each other's company.

We all squeezed into one tent and made Nescafé on the camping stove but no one wanted to sing or talk. Richard and Pauline were thinking about Brahms or each other, I was not sure which. I wanted to think over my conversation with Bill and work out what he had really meant. But Bill himself insisted upon opening a bottle of wine and saying at intervals: 'What are two letters that signify perfection? M – A – Emma,' (which was another quotation from Jane Austen) in a way that I felt to be particularly insincere. So I was quite glad to escape into our tent and wriggle into my sleeping bag. Just as I was dropping off to sleep Pauline arrived and I asked her politely:

'Did you have a nice evening?'

'Oh Emma, it was fabulous.'

'Brahms or Richard?'

Pauline giggled.

'Both, of course.'

The next day we set off for Brno, Czechoslovakia.

Chapter Thirteen

WE had booked places at a camping-site a few miles outside Brno where the river has been dammed to make a huge lake, big enough for sailing-boats and even steamers, surrounded by spruce and pine forests. Here and there people had holiday cottages, anything from straightforward wooden huts like chicken coops to fancy villas with verandas. We had been able to pay for our site and one meal a day in London.

When we arrived, Bill started saying 'please' and 'thank you' in Czech but it turned out that the girl in charge could speak a little English. She showed us the cafeteria and the washrooms and we soon had our tents pitched on a grassy headland overlooking the lake. Obviously the first thing to do was to have a swim in order to recover from our long hot dusty drive.

'It will save washing too,' said Richard, setting off at a furious crawl.

Pauline was winding her hair into a bathing-cap. 'How sensible you are, Emma, to have short hair,' she sighed, because I never bothered to wear a cap. I remembered then, guiltily, that I had not looked into a mirror lately to see how my hair was standing up to the rigours of foreign travel.

'I expect I look awful,' I said hopefully but by this time she had set off in pursuit of Richard. Bill, of course, insisted on doing a flashy dive from the rocks. I edged in slowly. You can never be quite sure with lakes. First there was mud and pebbles and then some sand which suddenly ended in a steep shelf and I found myself swimming. The water was warmer than in Salzburg. To me, used to the icy water on Stranday, it was almost lukewarm. Then some of the other campers who were also swimming started playing with a beach ball and soon we were all involved and it did not really matter what language we were talking.

We swam for hours without feeling cold, and then lay on our grassy headland, drying off.

'Isn't it blissful without the tourists,' said Pauline.

'But surely, they are all tourists here too?' I said puzzled.

'Ah, you have missed another salient point about tourists,' Bill explained lazily. 'Tourists are only objectionable when they speak the same language as oneself, ie, English or American. These tourists speak German, French, Italian, Czech and no doubt Serbo-Croat, therefore they are not tourists. They are just foreigners.'

'And very nice too,' grunted Richard, 'especially that blonde in the pink bikini.'

'What say we investigate the night life of old Brno?' Bill went on.

'Too tired,' grumbled Richard.

'Much too tired,' agreed Pauline.

'What about you, Emma?'

The thought of getting up, changing into a dress and trying to put on make-up with the help of a pocket mirror was too much for me. I shut my eyes and floated away.

So in the end we went, rather late, to the cafeteria and had soup and hard-boiled eggs surrounded by all sorts of salad, followed by horrible black coffee. Richard and Bill drank big glasses of cold beer – 'Pivo,' Bill had said, showing off his Czech – while Pauline and I had some nameless sort of fizzy drink that was called orangeade and quite clearly wasn't.

Afterwards we walked slowly back to our tents, listening to groups of campers in their red and blue track-suits, singing songs in different languages or playing transistor radios. Just to show that we were everyone's equal we gave a selection of our repertoire before we turned in.

Brno is on a river and surrounded by round smooth hills covered with forests. I suppose it must be roughly the same size as Edinburgh, and like Edinburgh it has an old city centre made up of tall crumbling stone houses. Then there were new suburbs with little houses and big blocks of flats, adjoined by green gardens full of apricot trees. There was a University and an industrial belt (which we did not bother to explore). But of course the architecture was quite different – the churches had onion-shaped domes more often than spires and the houses had flat roofs. So while Edinburgh is all spiky, Brno was mostly square. One bit of river had been turned into a municipal swimming-pool with a restaurant under the trees, but we did not swim there as the water was the colour of pea soup. Instead we sat under the trees and had ice cream and beer and made rude remarks (in low voices just in case anyone should understand English) about the fat women in skimpy two-piece swimsuits, who walked about quite unselfconsciously carrying plates of sausages or ice cream. The Czechs seemed to eat all day.

We walked in the market square where peasants were selling fruit and vegetables – mounds of golden apricots which looked beautiful but so often tasted like cotton wool, green peppers, beans, little ridge cucumbers and tomatoes. We bought food to take back to camp but it was extremely difficult because of kilograms. Only Bill seemed to have the faintest idea how much of anything to buy.

'That's because he has a computer instead of a brain,' jeered Richard.

'I have a computer as well as a brain,' said Bill smugly.

We had to rely on him, too, to work out some sort of relationship between pounds and kronen which again was difficult, firstly because they gave us a tourist rate which was nearly twice as much as the official rate, and secondly because while some things were much more expensive, others were much cheaper. We had to buy at least one meal a day, as well as drinks and ice cream, Pauline and I wanted to take back a few presents, and then there were the Festival tickets to buy. It was going to be a close shave so Bill and I decided to be generous and let the others have the lion's share of the music.

'But Emma has to be educated,' said Richard.

'A beautiful girl like Emma doesn't need to be educated,' Bill said slyly.

I fumed but said nothing. Because if I replied that even beautiful girls needed educating, then Richard would pounce on me for leaving school.

We had a lovely time in Brno. We used to get up early – everyone in Czechoslovakia seemed to start the day at about six-thirty. But with the sun shining and the air smelling sweetly of water and pine needles and the pigeons singing in syncopated rhythm, it did seem a crime to stay in bed. So we used to have an early morning swim and then make our own breakfast of fruit and bread and Nescafé because none of us liked the coffee at the cafeteria which was very strong and very black. After breakfast we would go into Brno to wander around with frequent stops for ice cream and beer. We visited the Anthropos Museum on the banks of the river and the mighty pleasure dome where the annual trade fair was held. We also went into one of the Baroque churches which was quite extraordinary. There were pictures and statues of saints in the brightest imaginable colours; mummies covered with velvet and jewels under glass cases; a long flight of steps leading to the altar flanked by huge blazing candles – we actually saw an old peasant woman going up these steps on her knees. Every inch of the wall seemed to be covered with murals and gold paint.

'Rather reminds me of the Odeon,' murmured Bill.

When there were chamber music concerts in the afternoon we ate at a restaurant, mostly slabs of meat with dumplings and cabbage. Otherwise we bought bread and cheese and sausage and had a picnic somewhere. There were lovely forest walks which led to little dusty villages, set about with plum and apricot trees and plots of maize and peppers. Most of the farms were cooperatives with big fields of corn or vegetables, but some still had strips of this and that which reminded me of my history books. There were vineyards, too, because this part of Czechoslovakia – Moravia – produces a lot of wine. Once we stopped to ask someone the way and it turned out that he spoke German. So we got talking and he took us into his little wine cellar and let us taste his icy cold white wine. He seemed to think that everyone in Britain was a millionaire and would not believe me when I told him that my family did not have a car.

In the evenings we mostly went to concerts or the opera.

The seats had turned out to be even cheaper than we had hoped so we could all go. But I found Janáček terribly difficult .to listen to. I could not understand how Richard and Pauline could come out raving and humming little bits to each other.

Then we would go home for supper and often we would have another swim before going to bed.

Almost before we had realized it, our ten days were up. We spent our last money having a slap-up lunch in the biggest hotel, the International, with Russian champagne – 'A little flashy but adequate,' said Bill – and bought presents to take home. The best shops for presents were those specializing in folk art, material, glasses, china and wooden toys. I bought a wooden cat for Vanessa, some little china figures of peasant women for Aunt Patsy and a bottle of plum brandy called Slivovic for Stephen. Pauline bought some beautiful liqueur glasses while the boys, who naturally hated shopping, sat in a pub drinking beer. Then, completely broke, we had a snack supper in the cafeteria where our fellow campers, who had mysteriously learned of our departure, started a farewell sing-song.

It was splendid hearing so many songs in different languages and when we were called to do our bit we sang about the horse and then about the nightingales. There was deafening applause for we gathered that in general the English are bad at singing songs.

'Emma and I are half Scottish, that's what makes the difference,' said Richard proudly.

Suddenly it seemed the right thing to go for a swim in the dark, so we all changed quickly into our swimsuits and bounced into the water, giggling and talking and bumping into each other. And of course when we came out we couldn't find our clothes and stumbled around shrieking with laughter, finding each other's sandals and towels.

After Richard and Pauline had gone off arm in arm for a last walk, Bill said to me:

'Are you in a sentimental mood, Emma? If so, let us also go for a moonlit stroll.'

We walked along a path in the opposite direction to Richard and Pauline, admiring the moonlight making little glittering triangles of gold on the black lake.

'I'll never forget this,' I murmured. I was in a sentimental mood.

'Neither shall I,' said Bill. 'In darkest computerdom I shall remember wandering on the shores of Brno lake with a beautiful damsel. What a pity you haven't got a dulcimer, Emma.'

'What a pity you haven't a guitar.'

'Yes, we could serenade each other.'

We paused and suddenly I was aware that lazy, nonsense-talking Bill had changed. He seemed to be giving off sparks of electricity and his face, in the moonlight, looked sharply angled instead of smooth. He took my hand, squeezing it hard, and then put an arm round me and I could hear his quick breathing.

'Oh Emma,' he said, 'you are nice. Do you like me?'

I pondered what he meant by the word 'like'. I did of course like him but I had a feeling he meant something different and that if I said: 'Yes, of course,' it would lead to misunderstandings. But I did not need to speak because he abruptly put both arms round me and kissed me.

It was very uncomfortable. Our teeth clashed (because I had been taken unawares) and my nose was squashed up against his cheek so that it was almost impossible to breathe. Oh dear, I thought, here I am beside a romantic foreign lake being kissed by a rich handsome clever young man and instead of being transported with delight I'm just thoroughly uncomfortable. I struggled free, gasping for air.

'I'm sorry,' I apologized. 'I'm not very good at this.'

'Never mind,' he said, 'you just need a little practice.' And he kissed me again, gently, which was much more pleasant. 'Let's sit down.'

I did not really like Bill kissing me but it seemed churlish to say so when he had always been so nice to me, quite apart from taking me out to an expensive dinner. In Edinburgh I had not been interested in boys and on Stranday there were no boys to be interested in, so I had no experience to judge if it was kissing itself I disliked or Bill personally. I tried to imagine Douglas saying, 'G-g-give me a k-k-k-kiss, Emma,' and then tripping over a tree root and I could not help giggling.

'What are you laughing about?' asked Bill crossly.

We were sitting close together and he had his arm round me and was kissing my neck in a tickly way.

'About a friend of mine with a stammer,' I explained unwisely.

'You shouldn't think about your friends when you're with me. You have no soul, Emma.'

'That's what Aunt Patsy says.'

He removed his arm and clasped his knees instead of me.

'You don't really like me, do you?' he grumbled, 'you're just being polite.'

'Of course I like you,' I replied nervously.

The trouble about kissing was that it had somehow dried up the conversation. In books Bill would have said: 'I adore you,' or 'You're the most beautiful girl in the world,' but in this case such remarks would have been untrue and absurd.

'How I envy you three,' said Bill suddenly in a low voice. 'You're all so sure of yourselves – as people I mean. No trouble in communication at all.'

I could hardly believe my ears.

'The trouble with me,' Bill went on, 'is that I've had dinned into my ears that it's unmanly to show my feelings until I've practically turned into a wretched computer.'

'Oh, what nonsense, Bill.'

'No spontaneity. But a chap would be crazy to walk in the moonlight with a girl and not try to kiss her, wouldn't he?'

'I suppose so. But I don't see why.'

I don't know if it was the wine he had drunk or the complete isolation of being alone in the black and white moonlit world that made him expand. But I realized now, for perhaps the first time, how utterly different Bill's private character was from his public one.

He told me about his parents, whom he did not much like – 'they just want me to conform to a pattern' – and how he had never met any girls except as people to dance with or to play tennis with.

'Surely at University it's different.'

'Oh, I've taken out a few but never made much headway.'

'I can't believe it.'

'I never know what to talk about,' he repeated.

'You're talking to me now and I like it.'

'So I am.' This apparently cheered him up and he pulled me to my feet and kissed me again. I liked it this time and it occurred to me that the reason was that I now knew him a little better.

We strolled back hand in hand and found Richard and Pauline sitting outside the tent, her head on his shoulder, both looking very sleepy and happy. We joined them and then, very softly so as not to disturb the other campers, we sang our song:

> *Alles schweiget,*
> *Nachtigallen*
> *Locken mit süssem Schall*
> *Tränen ins Auge*
> *Wehmuth ins Herz.*

which Bill had translated for me:

> *All is silent,*
> *Nightingales*
> *Bring with sweet melody*
> *Tears to the eyes and*
> *Grief to the heart.*

Chapter Fourteen

BILL did not talk to me again like that. He resumed his old habits of being gay and absurd and though he kept calling me 'sweet Emma' and 'beautiful Emma' and told me that he would teach his computer to write poems in my praise, I knew quite well that he did not mean a word of it. When we reached London he drove us direct to Pauline's house and left us there; he had an urgent appointment, he said. He kissed Pauline and me with light brotherly kisses, promised to meet us all soon, called 'Bung ho!' to Richard, and scorched off into the traffic.

In Pauline's house we sat around in a disjointed way, babbling to her mother about what a marvellous time we had had, what the weather and the food had been like, what a splendid driver Bill was and how the car had not broken down once.

Pauline's mother admired our tan, exclaimed over the liqueur glasses, insisted that I had grown and offered us drinks while she went to inspect the larder.

It is a curious feeling coming back from holiday. You feel a mixture of excitement and anti-climax. You want to describe your activities but it is somehow impossible to give more than the barest platitudes and statements of fact, like: 'Oh yes, we swam every day,' and 'Yes, the weather was marvellous,' which left all the important things unsaid. This useless sort of conversation continued all through supper. Richard, who is never any good at small talk, sat silent and thoughtful and I began to want very much to be somewhere I could feel at home.

'Let's have some music,' said Pauline at last.

'Yes, we've never played to Emma,' said Richard, brightening.

'We'll go upstairs if you don't mind, Mummy,' Pauline suggested.

'Yes, do, there's a TV programme I particularly want to watch,' agreed her mother, who was not musical and fortunately did not pretend to be.

Pauline had a lovely room on the first floor with long windows opening on to a little iron trellised veranda, overlooking the garden; she had a grand piano, a divan bed covered with cushions, lots of books in a glass-fronted bookcase and some gilt music stands.

She took out her oboe and started tuning while Richard did some flashy arpeggios on the piano.

'Lordy, my fingers are stiff,' he grumbled.

'What shall we play?' asked Pauline.

'The In Memoriam sonata,' said Richard.

I flashed a look of inquiry and dismay at him but he took no notice and bent his head over the keys while Pauline got out the music and arranged it on a stand. I curled up on the divan, feeling apprehensive. In general I found it easier not to think directly about my mother and father and knowing that this music had been written in their memory was in itself disturbing.

I am never sure what music is supposed to mean and it is possible that if I had just heard Richard's sonata out of the blue it might not have meant what it did on this occasion.

I know, too, that it is impossible to describe music in words because it has a language of its own.

The first movement was very strange – it was as if the oboe and the piano were fighting. The oboe would start a delicious tune full of life and gaiety and then the piano would spoil it with discords and savage rhythms. And I found myself understanding that this meant war and accidents and poverty spoiling people's happiness.

The second movement was entirely different, very slow and solemn, with long-drawn-out yearning melodies on the oboe against a continuous rippling piano-part like waves falling monotonously on the seashore. And I understood that this meant sorrow, but peaceful sorrow, no sadder than autumn when the leaves fall from the trees.

Then, in the third movement, the oboe brightened up and the piano joined in, still gayer and more boisterous. Sometimes the chords were harsh but the rhythms, instead of being savage and bitter as in the first movement, were energetic and hopeful. It ended in a triumphant cascade from the oboe while the piano rumbled like a drum.

As well as listening – or trying to listen – to the music, I was realizing why Richard was playing it for me. He was never much good at talking about his feelings but this was his way, not only of reconciling himself to death as well as life, but of telling me to do the same. Though he always seemed so calm and sure of himself as my big brother, he must have suffered as I had done. But while I behaved in a psychological way, he had written this gorgeous sonata, I wished I could express myself in some musical way, too.

When the sonata ended Richard looked up and saw my face. He came over and put his arm round me.

'And I said you weren't artistic,' he mumbled, 'I apologize. Well, what do you think?'

I could not answer for a minute but I managed to smile.

'It's marvellous,' I said. 'It says – oh, everything.'

'Not everything,' Richard said, 'not everything by a long chalk. But something.'

'Don't be sad, Emma,' said Pauline, undoing her oboe.

'I'm not sad – really – it's just–' I stumbled for words. I wanted to explain how much more complicated life was than I used to think; that I was beginning to understand that happiness was only an equal part of life with sadness; that if you are fond of people you have to be prepared to suffer.

'Anyhow, you think it's good, do you?' Richard asked.

'Oh Richard, you know I don't know anything about music.'

'You dare to say that after an expensive musically educational holiday,' he spluttered.

'OK, then. I think it's good.'

He smiled and went over to shut the piano and put the music away.

'When do you want to go back to your mad island?' he asked, 'or do you want to stay here for a few days?'

'You can stay here, honestly,' added Pauline.

'Will you be coming too, to Stranday?'

'Nope. We're going to a summer school. And then I must do some work.'

Suddenly I was longing to see Aunt Patsy and Stephen and Vanessa again and we discovered that if I caught the night train to Glasgow I'd be in Oban in time for the (summer schedule) twelve o'clock boat.

'Do you want to ring up?' Pauline suggested.

'No telephone.' Then I thought. 'But I could ring up the hotel and hope that the postman is there so he can take a message in the morning.'

'That sounds complicated.'

'It isn't complicated at all. It's perfectly simple,' I retorted, already feeling myself an islander with all our island customs to defend.

'The telephone's downstairs,' said Pauline helpfully.

When I got through to the Ardloch Hotel it was wonderfully satisfying to hear Mrs Innes' highland voice.

'This is Emma,' I said. 'Do you think anyone will be going by the cottage tomorrow? Is Roddy in the bar?'

'Surely,' said Mrs Innes. 'But if he isn't, someone can easy give him a message.'

'Would you tell him to tell my aunt that I'll be on the twelve o'clock boat tomorrow?'

'Do you want to speak to him yourself?'

'No, you see I'm ringing up from London.'

'London!' said Mrs Innes, thoroughly impressed.

I thought affectionately of my island which was like a friendly family in which everyone was used to helping everyone else. I imagined Roddy roaring along the shore road on his motor-bike (he is the postman) and stopping at our cottage to call out:

'Your niece is back from foreign parts, Mrs McTaggart, she'll be on the boat tomorrow,' and Aunt Patsy replying: 'Thank you, Roddy, have you time for a cup of tea?' Oh, how I was longing to get back.

Richard and Pauline took me to the station in a taxi, bought me some magazines and installed me in a half-empty carriage where they hoped I'd have a chance to lie down because although I had five pounds left of my holiday money I did not want to waste it on a sleeper.

'I wish you were coming too,' I said, quite sincerely, 'do come and visit soon, Pauline.'

'I'd love to, Emma. And you must come to Edinburgh.'

'We might manage a weekend towards the end of August after our summer school,' said Richard. 'In the meantime, be a good girl.'

I knew very well what he meant by being a good girl although he had been most scrupulous about not once mentioning school to me while we had been away.

He and Pauline stood arm in arm on the platform while I stood at the carriage door. How lucky they were to like each other so much. Then we all spoke at once saying, 'Bye' and 'See you soon' and 'Love to all' before doors were slammed, the whistle blown, and the train began to creak out of the station. I waved until they were out of sight and then retired to my carriage.

The journey was horrible but I was too happy and excited to mind much. And this state of suspended animation lasted until the boat drew up at Ardloch jetty and I looked anxiously to see if anyone had come to meet me.

Yes, there was Stephen in his navy-blue fisherman's sweater, waving frantically, and a few minutes later I was hurling myself into his arms.

'Stephen! How is everyone? How is Vanessa? How's the gallery? Have you sold any more pictures? Where's Aunt Patsy?'

'You look terrific,' said Stephen, not replying to any of my questions, 'simply terrific. Brown as a coffee bean and tall as a runner bean. It's lovely to have you back.'

'It's lovely to be back.'

'We'll go home on the minibus. I've bought some stores and besides, Patsy can't wait.'

'I can see you've had a good holiday,' said Donald grinning, humping assorted parcels and luggage on to the minibus.

'Oh I have,' I said happily, Stephen sat down beside me, assuring me repeatedly that Patsy was fine, Vanessa was fine, the weather had been vile, the gallery was ticking along nicely, they were fiendishly busy, the island was overrun with archaeologists as well as tourists and he was planning a one-man exhibition in Glasgow in the spring.

'And you, Emma, did you really enjoy yourself? No more island blues?'

Island blues? I had almost forgotten I had ever suffered from them.

'Salzburg was just as you described it,' I said. 'Did you get my postcard? I wrote it in the Glockenspiel Café. And Brno was fabulous – a huge lake full of luke-warm water – we swam twice a day and stayed in for hours. Pauline's awfully nice, rather beautiful really. I heard her play the oboe in London. She and Richard might come up to visit us later in August.'

When Donald drew up at our road-end Aunt Patsy was there to meet us, with Vanessa in the pram. The moment I had hugged Aunt Patsy I dived into the pram.

'She's huge,' I exclaimed, 'and what a lot of hair she's got. Vanessa, darling, I can't wait to cuddle you.'

Vanessa, disappointingly, not only did not smile at me but looked decidedly alarmed at my overtures.

'She's forgotten me already,' I grumbled.

'Well, I haven't,' said Aunt Patsy, 'though I must say you look amazingly different. Can you have grown? Perhaps it's your hair, but you look quite grown-up.'

We crowded into the cottage and there was a meal actually ready on the table, cold ham and lettuces from the garden, brown bread and honey. Glancing out of the corner of my eye I could see that the kitchen was unusually clean and tidy. Aunt Patsy had made an effort, specially for me.

'Now tell us,' she said, pouring tea, 'absolutely everything. Start at the beginning.'

Telling them absolutely everything was so much easier than talking to Pauline's mother that it lasted all through tea, was interrupted by Vanessa's bedtime – she kindly allowed me to bath her – and continued afterwards until as a grand climax I gave them their presents.

'Slivovic,' said Stephen. 'Is this guaranteed to send us reeling to bed?'

'Not in small quantities.'

'Then let us have a small quantity.'

'I'd sooner have wine,' I said, 'if you have any. I drink quite a lot of wine nowadays. You see, Pauline's mother told us not to drink water.'

'An admirable reason,' said Stephen, finding a bottle and pouring me out a glass.

'Let us drink to Queen Emma with thirty times three,' said Aunt Patsy. 'So you approve of Richard's choice, do you?'

'Oh yes.'

'And what about Bill? Did you fall for him?'

'Certainly not,' I said indignantly.

'Why not? You said he was rich and handsome and intelligent.'

I had not, of course, told them about the scene by the lake.

'He wasn't' – I paused, looking for a word – 'warm. He was terribly good company, gay and funny and kind, but – sort of buttoned up, if you know what I mean.'

They knew exactly what I meant.

'Your young man here has been asking for you,' said Aunt Patsy slyly.

'Who?' But I blushed. I knew perfectly well whom she meant.

'Alastair.'

'Oh, Alastair.'

'Yes, he's been round several times to ask when you were coming back.'

'Oh,' I said nonchalantly and then, swiftly changing the subject, 'Now it's your turn to tell me everything.'

Chapter Fifteen

THOUGHTS of Alastair had crossed my mind once or twice while I had been away. In fact I had even sent him a postcard from Brno. But after all I had only met him once so it was quite wrong of Aunt Patsy to call him my young man. That was a horrible expression in any case. I could hardly remember what he looked like and I felt shy at meeting him again.

So I made elaborate excuses about not really wanting to go on the dig; I said I would prefer to help in the gallery; that I would look after Vanessa and give Aunt Patsy a chance to get on with her own work; that I had had a marvellous holiday, and it was now my turn to buckle down to the chores.

'Nonsense, Emma,' said Aunt Patsy, 'we have a student to look after the gallery and Vanessa is no trouble at all now.'

'But—'

'You have to report at eight o'clock.'

'But I don't even know where they're digging.'

'You turn left at the burn and it's about two miles up in the hills just before you get to the loch. They've made a rough track and I daresay one of the Land Rovers will give you a lift.'

'Don't bully me,' I grumbled. 'Oh well, if I have to get up at an unearthly hour you'd better lend me the alarm clock. And I suppose I'll need sandwiches.'

'No, you won't. There is a mobile canteen.'

'Suppose it rains?'

'The glass,' said Stephen, 'is going up. You've brought some Central European weather with you.'

So the next morning I dressed in jeans, a cotton shirt and sneakers, put a jersey and an anorak into my rucksack – because barometers cannot be trusted on Stranday, which has weather rules of its own – and was just drinking a cup of coffee and eating bread and honey, when I heard a car hooting. Dashing out with my bread in one hand, I saw a Land Rover stopping at our road-end. Someone was waving. I waved back, raced inside for my rucksack and hurried up the track.

The Land Rover was chock-full of people but someone had opened the back and was standing waiting for me. It was, yes, it was Alastair.

'Hello, Emma,' he said, 'I heard on the bush telegraph that you were back so we thought we'd give you a lift. You are coming, aren't you?'

'Of course,' I said.

He helped me in, slammed the door and the Land Rover roared away.

'This is Emma, everyone,' Alastair introduced me. 'Emma, this is Peter and Carol and Ruth and David and Nancy and – oh, everyone.'

Everyone said 'Hi' or 'Hello' but since we were all crammed together it was difficult to see who was who. I looked sideways at Alastair and discovered that I did remember what he looked like, his thin face, bright-eyes and his quick eager way of talking. But whereas before he had looked pale and tidy, now he was tanned, his hair was shaggy and he wore a dirty blue shirt with a tear in it.

'I see you've had your hair cut,' he whispered.

'I see you haven't,' I returned smartly.

'Did you have a good holiday?'

'Marvellous.'

'Thanks for the postcard.'

'Where did you go?' asked one of the girls.

'Czechoslovakia,' I said grandly.

'Lucky you.'

Everyone talked at once and since they had had two weeks of working together their conversation was so full of private jokes and allusions and references to unknown people and things that I found it difficult to join in. But I consoled myself by thinking that if any of them had joined Richard and Pauline and Bill and myself, our conversations would have been just as difficult to follow.

At this moment we turned left up a rough track along the side of the burn. I had walked there once before but now it had been widened and was pitted with track marks. There was rough moorland on either side at first, which gradually grew steeper until the burn was only a thread of silver far down below in a narrow gorge. There was a stone wall ahead and here the Land Rover turned right and stopped beside a big bell-tent, another Land Rover and several crude notices saying 'Meter parking only' and 'Breathalyser testing station' and so on.

'We walk the rest of the way,' Alastair said, leading the way through a gap in the wall.

'What exactly shall I be doing?' I asked, hurrying after him. I did not want to make a fool of myself my first day.

'Light donkey work.'

'Such as?'

'Oh, carting the earth away or sieving it.'

'What do you do?'

'I dig with a teaspoon, no, actually it's a builder's pointing trowel.'

'What have you discovered so far?'

'A stone circle, Middle Bronze probably. We haven't found the burial chamber yet. That's when it will start getting exciting. A skeleton or two is always fun.'

We had been walking in twos up a steep path overhung with hazel and birch with very little chance of seeing where we were going, though we caught occasional glimpses of the burn and heard the tinkle of a waterful. Then the trees stopped, the gorge widened into a big grassy glen, with the moorland rising steeply towards Stranday's two mountains in front of us, holding the loch between them. This was where the excavations had been started.

The first day our activities were far too complicated for me to understand. I just had a confused impression of trenches, holes and sections; of young men in shorts or jeans with bright tattered shirts, some with 'Keep Britain Celtic' or 'Join the Beaker People' scrawled on them, and silly woollen hats with bobbles; of beefy girls in shorts and sun-tops carrying plastic buckets; of people wheeling barrows; of a little bird-like man with a pith helmet darting about uttering shrill cries of encouragement or censure; of a tall man with dark hair in a pudding-basin cut, scribbling away furiously in a notebook; of miscellaneous people with ranging poles, notebooks, tape measures and spirit levels.

But over the next few weeks, by listening, asking questions and borrowing books, I gradually got a picture of what was going on.

The dig was not one of those famous national excavations like discovering King Arthur's Camelot. As Mr Kilpatrick had told me, it was only a small field party, organized by the Archaeological Department of Glasgow University. In charge was Professor Dickinson, the small bird-like man, whom we naturally called Dickybird. The man with the pudding-basin hair-cut was a senior lecturer, nicknamed Pluto, who was responsible for notes and diagrams and the general keeping of records. There were in addition about twenty students and a few volunteers of whom I was a humble one and Douglas rather an important one as he took all the photographs – and everything had to be photographed with immense precision. Mr Kilpatrick worked with Pluto. He was having the time of his life, poking and peering, talking learnedly about geological strata, and comparing the University's discoveries with his own.

Apparently there are a lot of stone circles in the Western Isles and this one had been accidentally spotted by a member of the mountain rescue team who had been flying over in a helicopter and had noticed a meaningful hump in the grassy glen. If there had been more funds, an instrumental survey would have been taken first and there would have been special machines to strip off the turf and top-soil, but this expedition was run on a shoe-string with the minimum equipment and paid staff. The students and volunteers did not get paid at all, they camped out in the school where Mrs Kilpatrick gave them the benefit of home-baking for supper and at midday we all got a meal of sandwiches, cake and tea.

I soon learned that in the middle of a stone circle there is often a burial chamber and when you discover the skeletons or bone ash or the jewellery, pottery or weapons that people were buried with, you can approximate roughly the period in history to which they had belonged.

But of course it is often more complicated than this because a camp or a fort might have been built before – or after – the site became a burial ground. You might discover skeletons or bone ash or weapons belonging to people who had been killed in battle, and would then have to decide who had been invaded by whom. According to Mr Kilpatrick, the Western Isles had a long history of invasions and foreign settlers – people from the mainland of Scotland and Ireland, Vikings and adventurers from even more distant parts had all left their characteristic tracks behind them through the ages.

The important thing, the Dickybird drummed into us, was not to start with a pre-conceived idea of what you were going to find, but to examine everything that came to light scrupulously and make your deductions from the facts at hand.

Sometimes an excavation is done in squares of about ten feet, leaving little passages for people to walk on or wheel their barrows along, but in this case it was being conducted in a big circle about thirty feet in diameter, divided into quarters. A trench was cut in each quarter first and a cross-section taken, with photographs and notes, and then the individual levels were removed one at a time. So at any given moment you could be working on, say, the third quarter at level five, and everything you found had to be correctly related to its quarter and its level.

'It's not what you find but where you find it that's important,' the Dickybird said about twenty times a day, 'We're not treasure hunters. We're historians.'

The most experienced people examined the sections before the trowel men started clearing them away one by one. The earth they dug was carried off in barrows (there were lots of jokes about barrow boys) or in buckets and then, just in case something of value had been missed, it was all sieved yet again before being finally disposed of.

As Alastair foresaw, I was on the sieves with three other girls – one for each quarter – and though at first I was buoyed up by the thought of discovering some significant chip of pottery (I had quickly given up the idea of finding golden brooches or jet necklaces) I soon had to resign myself to a humdrum task that was not in itself more interesting than gardening.

And yet it was. Because it was run by the University, Dickybird used to stop proceedings every few days to give impromptu lectures on what we had discovered so far and what it all meant. He was a funny little man with a shrill voice but he sizzled with so much enthusiasm that it was impossible not to feel enthusiastic too.

'It is rather like trying to reconstruct a piece of music from a few scattered phrases,' I wrote to Richard. 'You'd have to decide if it was a symphony or a mass and at what period it was written. Then you'd need to imagine what the rest of the piece would have been like; and you'd have to discover what sort of instruments, who played them and in what circumstances. Out of a bit of a minuet, for instance, you'd have to build up a whole picture of ladies and gentlemen in wigs and furbelows dancing in a drawing-room to the harpsichord in eighteenth-century Vienna.

'We dig up a stone or a fragment of pottery or a film of white wood-ash invisible, I assure you, to the naked eye, or three stones together – one or two wouldn't be significant – and then the archaeologists go mad with enthusiasm.

'I hoped I'd be turning up golden brooches (lunulae!) and exotic jewellery, ha ha, but so far I haven't found anything. Still, the stone circle is beginning to appear. It's weird and wonderful and I can't wait to see my first skeleton.

'Do you remember the rather nice bloke called Alastair who came to the gallery opening party?'

Chapter Sixteen

Life was not all digging. We worked from eight until four so that there was time to go swimming afterwards. The students went back to the school for supper but I did not join them except sometimes for evening parties.

The more I saw of Alastair the better I liked him. No, that is an understatement, I was wildly in love with him. Every morning I woke up with the joyful knowledge that I would soon be in his company again. Every lunchtime I tried to arrange to sit next to him. Every day when we knocked off I hoped he would say: 'Are you coming swimming, Emma?' or 'What about biking to the school tonight, we're going to have a party?' And if he didn't I would sit at home straining my ears for the sound of footsteps which would mean that he was dropping in for a coffee.

The trouble was that I hardly ever saw him alone. We were always in a gang and he seemed to like it that way.

There was one particular girl I became terribly jealous of because she worked in his quarter while I was yards away up the hillside with my sieve. Her name was Nancy and she was one of those girls who always look immaculate however dirty the work is. She wore the briefest possible shorts with either a sun-top or a denim shirt and she was cooked a delicious golden brown, in contrast to me who had a perpetually peeling nose. She had charming ragged black hair, hazel eyes and a very faint lisp which I tried to despise but really thought was very attractive. And there she was working beside Alastair all day, laughing and chattering, getting him to light her cigarettes and laying her hand on his while he did so, while I watched miserably from afar. At lunchtime she always succeeded in sitting next to him – which I rarely managed – and she would do little intimate things like borrowing his teaspoon to stir her tea or begging him for a bite of his apple. She hardly ever spoke to me or tried to include me in the conversation and once I overheard her telling another girl something about 'Alastair's little lamb' which I was convinced referred to me.

So I became more and more self-conscious and tongue-tied. I watched Alastair closely but I could not be sure what his reactions were to Nancy's attentions. He laughed and talked to her certainly but he did not appear to make any special effort to wander off alone with her as the other couples did. Still, it was only reasonable that he found her more attractive than me. She was older, prettier, taller, cleverer, more amusing, I listed gloomily, and what is more she was packed with sex-appeal while I obviously had none at all.

How unfair it was, I thought, that I had not found it difficult to be gay and amusing with Bill whom I did not specially care for, while with Alastair, whom I adored, I was dumb and shy. If only I had been alone with *him* that evening in the moonlit forest beside Brno lake. He would surely have kissed me because Bill said men always did if they found themselves alone with a girl. How did I know that he didn't take Nancy for moonlight strolls and kiss her? I shuddered at the thought. Perhaps his invitations to me to go swimming or to parties were just kindness on his part. Little lamb indeed!

Of course I was not unhappy and jealous all the time but every day I became more and more obsessed with the idea of getting Alastair alone and testing his reactions. Aunt Patsy solved the problem for me by saying casually:

'Why don't you ask Alastair to supper some time, Emma? Not today because we've only got three chops, but tomorrow if you like.'

'I'll see,' I said cautiously.

'I know I can't compete with Mrs Kilpatrick as a cook but I could put my best foot forward.'

Now the difficulty was in getting out of everyone's earshot in order to give him the invitation, because if he refused I would be humiliated for ever and ever. It was impossible in the Land Rover. It was impossible walking to the site because he got into an argument with David. It was impossible at lunch. It grew more and more unlikely as the day wore on since, as it was cold and grey, we could hardly go swimming. I sieved mechanically, almost forgetting to keep my eyes open for significant chips or bits of bone. The afternoon crawled by and I thought four o'clock would never come. Eventually, however, Pluto blew his whistle and I saw to my delight that Nancy had scurried off leaving Alastair still hard at work. I strolled over as casually as I could.

'Doing some overtime?' I asked nonchalantly.

'I'd like to but it's not allowed. Dickybird doesn't trust us on our own.'

'My aunt wondered if you'd like to come to supper some time, tomorrow for instance.'

'That would be great,' said Alastair enthusiastically, smiling his special smile that always turned my bones to water. 'What time?'

'You could come straight home with me. You won't want to walk both ways.'

'I'll be a bit grubby.'

'Aunt Patsy won't mind. You can wash at the cottage.'

'If it's fine we could swim.'

I was transported with joy. I did not mind that Nancy sat next to him in the Land Rover. Tomorrow he would be all mine.

But – and it shows what a nasty character I have – my greatest triumph was when, going home the next day, I heard Nancy saying to Alastair: 'We're going to the pub tonight for a booze-up. You'll escort me, won't you?' and Alastair replying: 'Sorry. I have a date. Emma's aunt has invited me to supper.'

She did not speak but her look expressed commiseration.

For a moment I saw an Alastair I had never seen before. His face froze and his voice was cold and deliberate.

'Emma and her family happen to be friends of mine.'

'Sorry.'

She looked round to see if I had overheard and I pretended I hadn't. But I had to turn aside to hide my grinning face.

So when the Land Rover stopped at our road-end Alastair got out first and then helped me. We waved and set off down the track together.

'That Nancy's a bit of a menace,' he confided.

'She's very pretty,' I said with an effort.

'Sex-pots,' said Alastair, 'are out of place on an archaeological dig.'

'Isn't she interested in archaeology?' I asked timidly.

'Nancy? Interested in archaeology?' Alastair snorted. 'Have you no eyes in your head, Emma? She's lucky I haven't slapped her down before. But when you're working with people you have to be civil.'

I beamed.

We had a swim and then I changed into my brown dress and made up my eyes while he washed and changed into the clean shirt he had brought with him.

We wandered into the gallery and talked to Stephen while Aunt Patsy put Vanessa to bed; we wandered back to the cottage and drank glasses of wine; I laid the table and made a salad to go with the mammoth shepherd's pie; Alastair began talking about neolithic habitations and Aunt Patsy and Stephen became immediately absorbed.

'There could easily be one on the shore here,' said Alastair. 'If I could only find a midden.'

'A midden?' asked Aunt Patsy, astonished.

'Animal bones, goats or sheep or cattle – even grains of cereal – fish or shellfish remains. It would be much more exciting than finding a burial chamber, they're two a penny.'

'Emma wants to discover a golden brooch,' said Aunt Patsy.

'Of course I don't,' I said indignantly. That had been ages ago.

'Still it would be nice if she did find something,' said Alastair. 'She's worked jolly hard. I wish I could say the same for all the other female members of the team.'

'What do you mean by that?' demanded Aunt Patsy, who was always hot-tempered on the subject of sex equality.

'Beg pardon,' said Alastair, 'but I was thinking of one

particular female who is determined to drive me insane.'

'Introduce her to me,' said Stephen, 'if she's pretty.'

'Oh, she is,' I said eagerly and wondered why they all laughed.

It is still light on Stranday almost till midnight; even after the sun goes down there is a soft glow in the sky and though the sea and the grass and the trees fade into different shades of grey you are still conscious of the colours underneath.

So it was very pleasant strolling along the road with Alastair in the half-light – he had asked me to go part of the way back with him. Suddenly my idea of luring him on to the shore and inveigling him into kissing me seemed absurd and unnecessary. Now I knew that he really liked me and did not like Nancy, I stopped feeling agitated and anxious. It was like the first time I met him when we had talked so naturally and easily together.

He told me that his father was a boiler-maker and that they lived in Glasgow in a horrible block of new flats where you could hear the neighbours sneezing next-door. He had a younger brother still at school. He was deeply envious of Richard having a flat of his own.

'Are you really not going back to school?' he asked.

'I'm sick of exams,' I explained, 'and people saying it doesn't matter really but . . .'

'What will you do instead? Travel round the world with a mobile fish-and-chip shop? Or study, or what?'

'I'll probably help in the gallery for a bit.'

'Somehow,' said Alastair, 'I don't see you as that sort of girl.'

It was terribly flattering to know that he thought of me as any sort of girl. I made an inquiring murmur.

'I don't see you in the arty-crafty world,' Alastair said thoughtfully.

'It's not arty-crafty,' I protested indignantly. 'Stephen and Patsy are both proper professional artists.'

'Oh all right, I apologize. But you're not, are you, an artist? I think of you as a serious sort of person.'

'Stephen and Patsy are serious.'

'I give up,' said Alastair ruefully, 'I'm saying one wrong

thing after another. All I mean is that you're serious in a different way. And I thought you were really interested in this archaeology stuff.'

'Oh, I am,' I managed.

'That's what I mean. And if you wanted to go in for it seriously you'd have to cope with endless dreary exams.'

'I don't know yet,' I answered sulkily.

'Och, Emma, don't take the huff. The trouble is I've had my father breathing down my neck for so long about the importance of a career – with a capital C – that I've forgotten some people just want to live – with a capital L. You're a lovely girl, Emma. I like you just the way you are. Honestly.'

We were standing on the bridge over the burn, which was where I was going to turn back, and I was so astonished by his words that I gaped at him silently. He put his hands on my shoulders and looked at my face as if he were searching for something. Then he stroked my hair. I just stood there not daring to move or speak, waiting until he kissed me. It was a completely different kiss from Bill's. I felt I had been waiting for it for months instead of days. It was warm and close and satisfying and not uncomfortable at all.

'I wish there was time to get to know you properly,' Alastair murmured, 'I know you're pretty and nice and cheerful and clever but – there are only a few weeks left – och, well – what the hell – you're nice. Goodnight.'

He picked up a pebble, shied it into the burn and bounded off up the road.

'Goodnight,' I called after him.

Chapter Seventeen

I THOUGHT that kiss would change everything; that Alastair would look at me in a special way the next morning when he arrived in the Land Rover to pick me up; that everyone would know instinctively that he and I were a couple; that there would be little sly looks of understanding; that he'd perhaps take my hand as we walked to the site and that certainly he'd say: 'What are you doing tonight?'

But he behaved absolutely as usual, neither more nor less friendly, and Nancy certainly had not changed her tactics.

'Did you have an exciting evening?' she asked sarcastically.

'Very pleasant,' Alastair replied without turning a hair.

'It was wild in the pub,' she said, 'someone was singing folk-songs in Gaelic.'

I sniffed in a superior way. I had heard Hamish's Gaelic folk-songs dozens of times.

'Hamish always does,' I said loftily.

It was one up to me but it brought no satisfaction because Nancy settled down in Alastair's quarter, wearing a new crimson T-shirt with matching shorts, and I had to go up to my sieve as usual.

I bent over it, hating everybody and everything. Perhaps Alastair regretted having kissed me and having told me that I was a lovely girl. It might just have been a normal male reaction to moonlight and meant nothing at all. I did not have enough experience to know.

The circle of ground that we were digging was not exactly flat and the quarter of soil I had been sieving was slightly higher than the rest. A man called Ron was in charge, a happy, slapdash sort of character, who spent a lot of time flirting with his helpers, singing and making jokes. Occasionally he would shout kidding remarks up to me and I would retaliate, but today I did not feel like it. I bent over my beastly sieve and felt like crying.

So it was sheer accident that I noticed something that was neither a pebble nor a chip of stone. In fact I almost threw it away. It was a little lozenge-shaped object showing, under its cover of dirt, a faint glassy glitter. Could it possibly be important, I wondered? Whom should I show it to? The Dickybird? Or Alastair?

But I should feel a terrible fool if the Dickybird put on his long-suffering expression and said: 'No, dear, you should by this time be able to recognize an ordinary sliver of quartz . . .'

And I should also feel a terrible fool if I showed it to Alastair – in front of Nancy – and he made a similar retort.

I put it in the pocket of my jeans until I could decide what best to do.

When the lunch break came I could not face going off with the others to the tent so instead I climbed a little way up the hillside and lay down thinking how unhappy I was. Everyone always said how marvellous it was to be in love. But to me, it wasn't marvellous at all. It was painful. It gave me a choked-up sensation like indigestion, a fluttery anxiety like I get before exams or going to the dentist. Instead of being able to speak my innermost thoughts to the person I loved, I could talk to him less easily than to a brother, an aunt or a friend.

'What's up, Emma, aren't you feeling well?'

Alastair was beside me, looking down with a worried expression.

'Headache,' I mumbled.

'Sorry about that. It's such a splendid day. And last night was such a splendid night.'

I sat up at that. My choked-up feeling and my fluttery anxiety had completely vanished.

Alastair was smiling, a warm, friendly, sympathetic smile.

'Actually,' I said, 'I wanted your advice. I found something this morning but it's probably not important.'

I dug my hand into my jeans pocket and produced the little lozenge. 'Could this be anything?' I asked.

Alastair took it, rubbed it clean and held it up to the light, looking puzzled. Then his eyes lit up.

'Good Lord, I believe it's a faience bead,' he said. 'Emma, you're a genius. I don't believe anyone has found one in Scotland before. It's Eygptian, you know, and it will mean – oh, all sorts of exciting things.'

'What, for instance?'

'Oh, that there's probably another burial chamber farther up the hillside. It must have been disturbed, looted by

Vikings perhaps. But the most important thing is that some-one somehow brought it here all the way from Egypt. We must show it to the Dickybird.'

'Honestly?'

'Come on.'

Now I wished I had not skipped lunch. It was extra-ordinary how I was always hungry at moments of high elation when I should have been thinking of more important things.

'You haven't got an apple, have you?' I asked sheep-ishly.

'I'll get you one,' and he took my hand and we walked down the hillside together.

I was the heroine of the day. Dickybird gave us a long lecture about faience beads and about how important it was for even the humblest excavator to check on every grain of soil, while I purred with embarrassment, munching a mammoth sandwich and an apple. Then he came over to me and gave me a short talking-to for not reporting my find immediately.

'But I wasn't sure, you see,' I mumbled.

'No one expects you to be sure, my child,' he reproved, 'but I'd rather be bothered twenty times a day over nothing than miss something important.'

'I'm terribly sorry.'

Although I was really interested in knowing what my find meant, I was even more excited to realize that Alastair still liked me. Darling Alastair, darling faience bead, I mur-mured to myself at intervals as the afternoon work pro-gressed. At four o'clock when the whistle blew he came over to me and asked:

'Any sign of the second burial chamber?'

'Not yet but Dickybird's examining every grain of earth himself – he doesn't trust Ron or me.'

'What are you doing this evening?'

'Nothing much.'

'Would your aunt put up with me again, do you think?'

'Aunt Patsy won't mind. There's always soup or eggs.'

'Sure?'

'Perfectly.'

So once again he got out of the Land Rover with me and we walked down to the cottage. Aunt Patsy did not appear at all surprised.

'Get yourselves something to eat,' she said, 'I'm busy.'

'Emma is today's celebrity,' said Alastair proudly, 'she found a faience bead.'

'Marvellous!' said Aunt Patsy abstractedly, not having understood a word.

'She may go down in archaeological history,' went on Alastair.

'Marvellous! Emma, dear, do you think you could possibly put Vanessa to bed? I absolutely must get some designs ready for tomorrow's boat.'

This was something I could have done without but I was too happy not to be agreeable. After all, I did enjoy putting Vanessa to bed, but not half as much as talking to Alastair, not a quarter as much, not an eighth, a sixteenth, a thirty-two'th as much.

'Sorry,' I said to Alastair. 'You can read the paper – if there is a paper – while I perform my duties.'

'That's all right. Actually I want to work on my notes.'

He settled down at the kitchen table with an absorbed air and started writing and drawing little diagrams while I collected my darling cousin and prepared her for bed. I wanted him to watch and admire but he took not the slightest notice of us.

Vanessa was on mixed feeding now and I had to stuff into her mouth some horrible mixture of pulverized vegetable, before giving her her bottle. She seized the spoon from my hand before each mouthful and tipped the contents down her bib. Then she looked up at me with a diabolical grin.

'Vanessa, you beast!' I remonstrated. Vanessa kicked out with one sturdy leg and almost overturned the mug of hot water which was warming the bottle.

I mopped her up with a wet flannel, changed her nappy and took her upstairs to bed. She could do without a bath for once, I decided.

When I finally came downstairs Alastair had disappeared.

I rushed to the window and saw him walking about by the edge of the shore. I brushed my hair but felt too chagrined to change into a dress.

'Now this would be a likely place for a habitation,' Alastair said thoughtfully when I arrived beside him, and proceeded to tell me why.

'Do you want some supper?' I inquired when I could get a word in.

'Supper? Oh yes, that would be nice. Give me a shout when it's ready.'

The nerve of him! I had worked hard all day. I had made an important archaeological discovery. I had put the baby to bed. And now I was expected to provide supper just like that. Alastair was just as bad as Richard and Aunt Patsy and Stephen, who were all inclined to go into a trance when they got interested in their work.

I scowled and walked sulkily back to the house considering what I should do to retaliate – wash my hair? write a letter? start reading *War and Peace*? I tidied up Vanessa's things gloomily, pondering on woman's lot, well, not so much woman's lot as my own. I was born to be downtrodden by the inspired dedicated few. I should have to find something of my own to be interested in if I wanted to survive. I went upstairs and seeing my history notebooks, I took one off my bedroom shelf. What ages ago it seemed since I had studied the reforms of the nineteenth century, Reform Bills, Education Acts, Factory Acts. And the whole nineteenth century was only yesterday compared with the burial ground up on the hills. And the neolithic habitation (if there was one) would be a couple of thousand years beyond even that. I fell into a reverie, imagining those early people perhaps actually living on the site of this cottage, eating fish and shell-fish and gulls' eggs, keeping goats and treasuring their – oh dear, I knew so little, did they have jewellery or not? I must ask Alastair to recommend some books – Alastair! I had honestly forgotten about him. I snapped the book shut and hurried downstairs to fry eggs and bacon.

'I'm getting awfully hungry,' Alastair said plaintively, 'I thought you'd forgotten about me.'

He got up from where he had been sitting at the table and put his arm around me.

'I'm starving,' he whispered into my ear, and then, much much later, 'is there anything I can do to help?'

'You may lay the table and cut the bread,' I said graciously, taking out the frying-pan.

Chapter Eighteen

SUDDENLY it was the middle of August and the day before my birthday. We had found the second burial chamber but it had been disturbed, the skeleton was not intact, and if there had been any jewellery – as my faience bead had suggested – it had been swiped. But though I was disappointed, I was too preoccupied with Alastair to bother very much. I saw him nearly every evening and I spent the days in anticipation, imagining what we would say to each other and how he would kiss me goodnight.

I should have been perfectly happy and yet I wasn't. It seemed that I wanted to be alone with Alastair much more than he wanted to be alone with me. He liked playing ball games on the beach with the crowd. He liked a lot of horseplay and splashing when he went swimming. He did not want to sit still for a minute and sun-bathing bored him. Even when I succeeded in luring him on to my rock he kept jumping up to hunt for moss agates, splitting open likely stones with a hammer borrowed from Mr Kilpatrick.

Even at the cottage he seemed to spend as much time talking to Aunt Patsy and Stephen as to me. So I kept worrying that I was not pretty or clever enough to please him.

And even when he put his arms round me and kissed me on the little bridge where we always said goodnight, he did not make the passionate speeches I was longing to hear – only 'Nice Emma', and 'I like you'.

I hoped that now I was sixteen he would treat me differently.

Aunt Patsy had promised a special birthday supper to which he was of course invited.

'As it's such a special occasion I'd better go back to the school and change,' he told me during the lunch break.

'Don't take too long.'

'I'll see if I can borrow a bike.'

While Aunt Patsy was putting Vanessa to bed I changed into my flowery dress and tried to bring some order to my hair which was disintegrating into its highland cattle-cut again. I looked disgustingly healthy and outdoor and un-romantic, I decided, staring gloomily at my peeling nose and my round weatherbeaten face. No wonder Alastair did not make passionate speeches. When would I ever become elegant and sophisticated and sexy?

I think it was at this moment that I realized I should have to go back to school. Otherwise how could I ever catch up with Alastair? He would go on getting cleverer and more knowledgeable and I should be left behind with no qualifications for anything except looking after babies and doing a bit of amateurish weaving and pottery. Aunt Patsy did not really need my help but as long as I was on the spot she would take advantage of me. As long as I had no proper work of my own I would continue to be Alastair's little lamb.

If only I did not have to go to Oban and stay in some ghastly hostel where we would probably be treated like de-linquents and forced to be in by ten o'clock ever night. And I would have to share a room with some snuffly schoolgirl and spend the evenings in a jolly common-room watching telly or playing card games. For two whole years of the precious five we were renting the cottage!

Still, I thought, cheering up, there would be holidays; Alastair could come for Christmas and we could go digging again next summer; and there *had* been that letter from Stephen's friend in America saying he liked it out there so much he planned to settle indefinitely . . .

I gave my hair a last desperate comb and went downstairs to help with supper.

We were having chicken cooked in wine with raspberries (our own) and cream to follow. Aunt Patsy had actually tidied the kitchen and laid the table already. At my place were three parcels.

'Goodie, goodie,' I said, dancing round the room, giving Aunt Patsy a hug as I passed her. It was all quite different from my birthdays in London, when I had always had a cake with candles, but I liked it this way too.

Stephen came in and kissed me.

'My, how elegant we are. How can we live up to this, Patsy?'

'Change your shirt, darling.'

'I'll do that. What time is Alastair coming?'

'I said not later than seven.'

So presently we were sitting in the civilized room, drinking wine, while Stephen played a record of Janáček's Sinfonietta to remind me of Brno.

'Here's to you, Emma,' said Stephen, raising his glass. 'What a lot of luck you've brought us.'

To cover my confusion I said briskly:

'I'm going back to school.'

'No one's been bullying you, have they?' asked Aunt Patsy anxiously.

'Not to speak of. It's just that – I really am interested in history and everyone knows I'm not artistic.'

'You haven't by any chance got ambitions to be an archaeologist, have you?' Stephen asked slyly.

'Well,' I said cautiously.

'Does that mean Oban?' Aunt Patsy asked.

'Yes. And it will be horrible. I know that perfectly well.'

'I don't know how we'll manage,' said Aunt Patsy dolefully. 'I'll get into bad habits again without your rigorous discipline.'

'I'll be home for holidays and long weekends,' I said quickly.

We fell into a companionable silence while I listened for Alastair. It was after seven and he still had not arrived.

At half past seven Stephen said:

'Look, I'm starving to death, I don't think we can wait any longer for your young man, Emma.'

I went out to look up the road but there was no sign of him. I was bitterly disappointed. I shut my eyes, counted a hundred and then opened them again. Still no sign. Suppose Nancy had lured him to the pub? Suppose his bike had a puncture? Suppose he had simply forgotten? Suppose . . . ?

I crawled back into the cottage, sat down at my place and tried to show enthusiasm over my presents.

Stephen had made me a beautiful copper medallion to hang round my neck on a leather thong – it would look perfect with my brown dress. Aunt Patsy had given me some perfume. The third parcel was from Richard, a book about archaeology and a long letter which I put aside to read later when I was in bed.

I thanked them both, slung my medallion round my neck, dabbed perfume behind my ears and began to eat the delicious food. But all I could think of was Alastair.

He arrived just as we were attacking the raspberries.

'I'm terribly sorry,' he said but did not explain the reason for his lateness.

He had brought me some chocolates which disappointed me as I had been hoping for something special that I could keep and that would make a link between us when he had gone away. And though he praised the food and admired my medallion I had the feeling that he was miles away.

After supper he sat silently looking into space and I became more and more upset. What could be the matter? Had he decided to chuck me? And then felt that he ought not to do it on my birthday?

At last he stood up and said:

'Do you mind if Emma and I go for a walk?'

'Of course not,' said Aunt Patsy.

We walked down by the shore in silence until at last Alastair turned to me and said:

'Emma, I've got to go back to Glasgow. Tomorrow, on the early boat.'

'Oh . . .' I couldn't speak.

'There was a letter from my Mum when I got back this afternoon. Dad's lost his job. The shipyard's sacked a whole lot of folk and he's one of them.'

Alastair always became very Scottish when he spoke about his home, as if he was slipping back into childhood ways of speech.

'Oh no,' I said sympathetically.

'If I go home tomorrow I'll be able to fix myself up with a job for the rest of the vac. To help out.'

'You'll not have to leave the University, will you?' I asked dismayed.

'Over my Dad's dead body. He'd never let me.'

'What will you do?'

'Labouring, I expect. Oh Emma, I didn't want to spoil your birthday. That's why I was so late. I had to make arrangements. And I thought we'd have another week together.'

'There's Christmas,' I said, though I felt more like crying. 'You're invited.'

'I'll have to see. There won't be much money to throw around.'

'Won't your father get another job?'

'Things are closing down all over,' said Alastair gloomily. 'My Mum's fair upset.'

It was true that living on an island did, to a certain extent, insulate you from all the awful things happening in the rest of the world.

I realized there was a whole chunk of Alastair's life about which I knew absolutely nothing. I had seen him absorbed in his digging, racing on the sands, playing the fool in the sea, joking with the other students, telling me I was nice and that he liked me. But I had never seen him at home, the clever responsible son of the family. I imagined him putting his arm round his mother and telling her not to worry – he'd see her right. And going out for a pint with his father, talking in dry half-sentences and cursing the Government.

'It's been the greatest holiday,' said Alastair, squeezing my hand, 'meeting you. But too short. Much too short. You will write, won't you?'

'Pages and pages and pages,' I said unsteadily.

'Tell me what you're studying at school.'

'Who said I was going back to school?'

'I knew you would.'

'How?'

'Because,' Alastair said grinning.

The rest of the evening sped by while I tried to hold the minutes back. I gazed at Alastair in order to memorize every detail of his face, to remember every word he said. And I shut my eyes to recall exactly how the grey sea was curling up the wet sand, how the moon slid in and out of the soft clouds; the smell of seaweed and drying hay, the sound of the waves and the wind in the trees, so that at any moment when I was alone I would be able to re-create every sight, smell and sound.

We kissed goodbye on the little bridge.

'Emma, don't cry,' he whispered.

'I'm not,' I lied.

'This is only the beginning.'

'I know.'

Eventually he walked away, turning round to wave every few seconds, and I stood there, waving back and feeling the tears roll down my cheeks. Then I turned for home.

The moment Aunt Patsy and Stephen saw I was crying, they gathered round me, poured me a cup of tea and made comforting remarks.

I had meant to be very stiff-upper-lipped and restrained but it was much warmer and more friendly to tell them how I really felt, knowing that they would not make stupid remarks about how young I was, how the time would dash by and it would be Christmas (or Easter or next summer) before I knew, and that I must cheer up. Instead they told me how nice Alastair was and how much they liked him. He was quite right to go home to help his Mum, it showed how mature and responsible he was.

'A strong character,' said Aunt Patsy, 'and anyone who has to cope with you, Emma, needs a strong character.'

'I have a strong character too,' said Stephen modestly.

At last I went to bed, a little comforted, but still wondering how I could endure the long weeks before I saw Alastair again.

Chapter Nineteen

I FELT too wretched the next day to go digging so Stephen kindly met the Land Rover on my behalf and said that I had to stay at home to get my things ready for school. He and Aunt Patsy were brisk and matter-of-fact at breakfast and took no notice when the occasional tear plopped on to my plate.

'We'd better see Michael Kilpatrick and find out what the drill is,' Stephen said.

'Another uniform, grrr,' shuddered Aunt Patsy. 'Stop it, Monster,' she told Vanessa who was sitting in her high-chair smearing Farex over her face.

What did it matter what I looked like, I thought drearily, with no Alastair there to see.

'I'll take Emma to Oban a couple of days before term starts,' suggested Stephen, 'to get her things and to inspect the hostel.'

Hostel! Ugh!

'If there's some dragon in charge,' said Aunt Patsy fiercely, 'I won't let her go. And that's that.'

I left the two of them making plans for my life in Oban and went upstairs to write to Alastair. I would have to wait until I received a letter from him before I posted it just in case I had said unsuitable things. I did not want to write 'Darling' Alastair if he wrote 'Dear' Emma or to say 'love and kisses' if he only wrote 'love'. It would be my very first love letter and it had to be exactly right. 'Dear, dearest, darling, gorgeous Alastair,' I composed in my imagination, 'I shall never forget yesterday evening, partly because it was so sad and partly because I really felt that you loved me.' But of course I would not write that at all. I would say: 'Dear Alastair, I hope your journey back was not too horrible, that you're cheering your Mum up and that your Dad will soon get another job. I miss you very much.'

I sat down at my table and shut my eyes to remember better every detail of yesterday evening – I was standing on the little bridge and Alastair's arms were round me and he was saying: 'Don't cry Emma' no, it was too painful. I had better think of something quite different.

I noticed the archaeology book Richard had given me and then I remembered – I'd never read his letter. I opened it and began to read.

'I hope this tiny gift arrives in time for your birthday,' he wrote, 'and that it will be helpful to your ploys. I couldn't understand a word of your last letter – what is a faience bead? You've got very learned all of a sudden. I haven't written lately because I've been completely embroiled in composing a meisterwerk, a quintet this time, for oboe, piano and strings. Janáček will have to look to his laurels.

'Rather tentatively and at the risk of being told I am interfering in your life, which of course is true, what plans are you making for your immediate future? I cannot help but think that with the common-sense for which you are famous you have decided to continue your studies. Now listen – you don't have to go to Oban. Why not come here, stay with me, and go back to Parkhill?

'I mentioned the matter to my landlady who has a bed-sitter, all chocolate brown paint and sick green curtains it is true, but still a room of your own. I'm sick of my own cooking. I promise to provide you with exquisite music if you provide me with delicious food. I suppose we shall squabble from time to time but Pauline has agreed to act as mediator. She thinks it's a great idea, by the way.

'Tell Patsy and Stephen that I shall watch over your (a) morals (b) health (c) spiritual welfare and (d) behaviour. There is to be no necking in the parlour or dancing in the streets.

'I have printed my telephone number at the top of this letter so that you can phone me immediately if you are coming. What do I mean "if"? "When" is a better word.

'I have just bought a little vintage motor car for £15, held together with pieces of string, india rubber bands and will-power – but it goes.

'Salud – Richard.'

I read this letter very slowly and then I read it through again. If I had to go to school, Parkhill would be better than a strange one. And I'd have a room of my own. It had been the idea of sharing which had made me so particularly dislike the thought of a hostel. I'd make new curtains and get rid of the chocolate brown paint. I would eat with Richard instead of with hordes of jolly girls. I'd do the housekeeping without any interference from anybody. I'd meet Pauline and Richard's other friends. My spirits rose a fraction of a degree.

But perhaps Aunt Patsy would not think it was suitable and would doubt Richard's ability to look after me. I must ask her quickly.

I tore downstairs to find that she and Stephen had gone into the gallery to work. Vanessa was sitting up in her pram, banging her pram beads and chuckling. I gave her a quick kiss.

'Listen,' I said, bursting into the gallery. 'Richard says why don't I stay with him in Edinburgh and go back to Parkhill.' I waved the letter at them.

Aunt Patsy snatched it from me and read it with Stephen leaning over her shoulder.

'I can go, can't I?' I pleaded. 'It would be so much nicer than staying in Oban.'

'Hmmm,' said Stephen.

'And lots of people get University places from Parkhill – I'm sure it's a better school.'

'Well,' said Aunt Patsy.

Then an awful thought struck me. Perhaps it would cost too much money. It would be far more expensive renting a bed-sitter and providing my own food than living in a hostel. I simply could not expect Aunt Patsy and Stephen to support me in a life of luxury while they ate nettles.

'B-b-but,' I stammered, 'perhaps it would be too expensive, I mean, I've only just remembered.'

I felt fearfully embarrassed. There had been the insurance money but I had no idea how much, or if it had already been spent.

'Of course you can go,' said Aunt Patsy quickly, seeing my confusion. 'And don't worry about the money. Unlikely as it may seem, we saved most of the insurance money for you just in case something like this happened.'

'Not enough for champagne every night,' said Stephen, 'but you shouldn't starve.'

'Then I can really go? Oh thank you, thank you terribly.' I hugged them both.

'This is a very happy solution,' said Stephen.

'I never wanted her to go to Oban.'

'I'd better go into Ardloch to phone Richard,' I said. 'Has anyone any sixpences?'

'I don't somehow think we're going to do any work today,' Aunt Patsy sighed, 'so let's give up the idea and have a celebration lunch at the hotel.'

'Agreed,' said Stephen, 'I don't feel like work anyhow. Too much excitement. Do you think you'll be hungry, Emma?'

I had not had any breakfast and I began to feel familiar pangs. I rushed back into the cottage to prepare a portable lunch for Vanessa. I knew quite well why I was hungry – it was because a glorious thought had just come into my head. Alastair lived in Glasgow and Glasgow and Edinburgh were only an hour apart.

Piccolo non-fiction

Piccolo All The Year Round Book 50p
Deborah Manley

Collecting Things 30p
Elizabeth Gundrey

Amazing Scientific Facts 25p
Jane Sherman

Blue Peter Special Assignment: Venice and Brussels 25p
Dorothy Smith and Edward Barnes

Blue Peter Special Assignment: Madrid, Dublin and York 25p
Dorothy Smith and Edward Barnes

Piccolo Encyclopedia of Useful Facts 50p
Jean Stroud

You can buy these and other Piccolo books from booksellers and newsagents; or direct from the following address:
Pan Books, Cavaye Place, London SW10 9PG
Send purchase price plus 15p for the first book and 5p for each additional book, to allow for postage and packing

While every effort is made to keep prices low, it is sometimes necessary to increase prices at short notice. Pan Books reserve the right to show on covers new retail prices which may differ from those advertised in the text or elsewhere

Piccolo fiction

Monica Dickens
Follyfoot 40p
Dora at Follyfoot 30p
The House at World's End 35p
Summer at World's End 35p
World's End in Winter 35p
Spring Comes to World's End 35p

Rudyard Kipling
The Jungle Book 50p
The Second Jungle Book 50p
Just So Stories 40p
Puck of Pook's Hill 50p
Rewards and Fairies 50p

Antoine de Saint-Exupéry
The Little Prince 35p